HUNTING THE TALL BLONDE
The Funny Detective – Volume 5

David Berardelli

HUNTING THE TALL BLONDE
The Funny Detective – Volume 5

FICTION4ALL

Chapter 1

Neil Haversack came to see me in my cell just two hours after I was arrested for murder.

It was after ten on Friday night, and Neil was not in one of his better moods. I couldn't blame him. Neil didn't like being hauled back to the Police Station just hours after he'd finished up a hectic work week dealing with surly cops and arrogant individuals in suits wanting him to do his job their way. Neil enjoyed spending his Friday nights at home in front of his widescreen, his feet propped up, a bottle of beer in his lap.

And he certainly didn't appreciate being called back in just an hour or so after he'd had his dinner and had just cracked open his second beer.

I hadn't seen my dead buddy Mike most of the evening. Luckily, she hadn't appeared in the cell with me. If she had, I wouldn't have been able to talk to her. The small black box fastened just above the door to my cell provided clear proof that I was being monitored. If anyone saw me talking to someone who wasn't there, they would have transferred me to Psych, shaved my head, clipped off my nails and put me on a diet of stewed prunes. I wouldn't have minded the nail clipping, but I liked how my hair looked and hadn't experienced a craving for stewed prunes since I was a toddler.

"Why the hell am I here, Deacon?" Neil barked at me the moment the guard opened the cell door.

Neil looked like someone who had been interrupted in the middle of his favorite part of the weekend. He was wearing a loose-fitting gray

5

sweatshirt with the number 24 on the front, frayed jeans and beat-up tennies—his bumming-around-the-house outfit—and his eyes were bloodshot. He stood stiffly, his hands on his hips, glaring as the sheepish-looking cop slammed the cell door shut and spun around quickly to watch the other end of the corridor and appear as invisible as possible.

"I called you," I told him.

He shook his head and glared. "You know what I mean, dammit."

I knew right then that being a smartass right now wasn't going to get me anywhere. If anything, it would probably earn me more jail time, so I told myself to cool it. I knew I was in hot water, so I figured this would be a dandy time to try out my people skills. Neil wasn't the perfect guy to try people skills on, but if I could manage it with him, it would most likely work on just about everyone else.

"They let me make one call, so I called you."

"Dammit, Deacon, you were supposed to call—
"

"I know. I just figured I'd try you first."

"Why?"

I shrugged. "We're buds, ain't we?"

"Tonight? I ain't so sure."

"We go way back, Neil..." I hoped that would cut some of the edge off his anger.

It must have. He sighed. "Just put a lid on the bullshit and tell me what happened." He shuffled over and collapsed on the hard cot beside me. "It's been a long night, a helluva long week, and I'm damn tired."

"I know. I'm going through the same thing."

6

He rubbed his eyes and yawned. Then he shook himself. "Is it true that you've been brought in for murder?"

"That's what they told me."

"They told me out there it was pretty bad."

"It was awful."

He sighed and rubbed his eyes again. Then he shrugged. "All right, then. Let's have it."

"Right now?"

He lowered his head and stared at the concrete floor for a few minutes. "No, Deacon. Let me get some shuteye here first. This cot looks a helluva lot more comfortable than the four-thousand-dollar job I just bought for the house. Then I'll have the Station manicurist come in so she can do our nails. Once she's through, you can tell me tomorrow afternoon. Better?"

"Seriously? You've got a manicurist here?"

"Dammit, Deacon..."

I knew right then that I was going to have to work a little harder on keeping my smartass down to lower simmer. It's really hard, though—especially when someone hands you so many possible zingers. People skills. I had to remind myself. "All right, I'll knock it off and get serious. It'll be tough, but..." I shrugged.

"Neither of us is getting any younger..."

"All right, then. Here's my story..."

Chapter 2

I'd had a rough week myself.

It probably wasn't nearly as bad as Neil's, but for me, it was still bad—but for a totally different reason.

The reason, of course, was that it had been a series of five long, boring days. I didn't mind the long part. Hell, I'd had a bunch of those over the years. All private detectives go through periods where the jobs just don't come in, sometimes for weeks at a time.

However, being bored was what usually put the kink in my colon. Boring, to an energetic private eye like myself, was the kiss of death, and often led to burnout and career change.

I'd had just two clients—which made me a little nervous about how I was going to come up with my next monthly rent check. Two middle-aged sisters had come into the office Monday morning, asking me to check out the whereabouts of some long-lost uncle who owed them money.

The case took me about four hours.

I warmed up my chair the rest of the week, took several short naps, drank coffee, tossed two or three hundred darts at the dartboard I'd bought a few months earlier, and watched the Orange Avenue traffic zip by my office window. My dead buddy Mike, bless her, broke the monotony a few times by materializing on my desk and entertaining me with her dry wit and impish moods.

Other than that? Four solid days of nauseating boredom had plagued me, making me wonder why I hadn't chosen a more exciting career, such as plumbing or garbage collection.

By five-thirty on Friday, I needed release from my suffocating cocoon of inactivity. I decided to drive over to Sheffield's on East Colonial, listen to some quality sounds, have a couple of drinks, and treat myself to a steak dinner at one of several restaurants just a few doors down.

Like most bars in the Central Florida area, Sheffield's hadn't been around very long. The business before it had been one of those fast-food eateries that pops up overnight, enjoys a great crowd for a few months, then folds when management discovers that the teens they'd brought in to run it had no sense of responsibility and, like so many of their peers, devoted more time to their cell phones and iPads than to their actual jobs.

Sheffield's catered to the older crowd, although many in the 25-35 age range frequently came in for their excellent club sandwiches. The place played all sorts of jazz and the sixties stuff I loved so much, rather than the mindless atonal rap crap with its jungle beat and vulgar street-barking that had turned the music business upside-down decades earlier.

Sheffield's owners apparently grew up listening to the Beach Boys, The Beatles, The Stones, Blood, Sweat & Tears, Chicago, Three Dog Night, and all those other classic rock groups popping up from the Woodstock era. My cup of tea, of course, but I knew better than let myself get too close. Having lived in Florida most of my life, I knew that once I let my guard down and made this place my regular haunt, Sheffield's would close up shop and morph overnight into another Beefy Broiler Bonanza, or Crispy Fries R Us.

At five-thirty, I left the office. At five-forty-five, I stepped into Sheffield's and, not expecting anything special or extraordinary to happen after nearly a solid week of excruciating boredom, chose a stool in the middle of the bar.

Then, as I nonchalantly scanned the darkly lit place, I saw her.

A blond goddess sitting about eight stools down, at the far end of the bar.

Like most men, my first instinct was to get her attention subtly, using my drop-dead good looks and devil-may-care attitude. Since there were other guys in the room and since I wasn't sure if any of them had tried the same thing before I came in, I figured the drop-dead good looks thing might not work. Besides, since I was now over forty, I wasn't totally sure how good-looking I was and didn't want to run the risk of having my ego bruised.

I was, however, pretty sure the devil-may-care attitude might work a little better. Babes seemed to prefer guys who didn't get worked up over a beautiful face and figure. They also seemed to respect a man possessing more than the average amount of self-control. From what I'd also observed, they didn't think too much of someone who drooled and went all sorts of clumsy. In my own personal unwritten book of sexual conquests,

I'd had much better luck when I gave the impression that I didn't care if I got laid or not.

Sheffield's bar lady, a good-looking redhead about fifty years old, came over and asked what I wanted. She was tall, about five-nine, with small boobs and a tiny waist. After I gave her my order, she said, "Any requests?"

The speakers were doing one of Chicago's earliest LP's. I saw no reason to interrupt the flow.

"No, thanks. Chicago's always been good enough for me."

When she came back with my drink, I said, "Do you always ask all your customers for requests?"

She smiled. "Just the ones who really appreciate what we play."

"Am I that obvious?"

"Well, we've seen you in here several times, and you always seem to enjoy what comes out of the juke, so…" She shrugged and wandered off.

I sipped my drink and hoped that her version of obvious wouldn't pop my devil-may-care bubble. I figured that since we were talking about my taste in music and not women, I was pretty safe. Besides, the goddess wasn't watching at the moment, so I breathed a little easier.

I sipped more of my drink. Just as I set down my glass, I saw that my goddess was getting up to leave.

It just figured. I'd planned to down at least one drink before deciding what to do about my approach. I realized that in this scenario, dragging my feet wouldn't get me very far. As far as I could see, she was the only babe sitting alone in the room.

And with more than a dozen guys sitting at tables, that narrowed down the playing field considerably. It also narrowed down my decision-making time.

However, I soon realized that none of that mattered. Right after she slid off her stool and picked up her clutch, she walked right over to where I was sitting. And stopped.

"Hi." It was a soft, low-pitched voice, and I heard it the same moment I smelled her strong ginger scent lightly brushing the air around my face.

She was just a couple of feet away, smiling timidly. She was even more beautiful up close—her eyes large and deep blue, with long, thick lashes. Her cheekbones were swelled, her lips full and pouty. She looked like the poster girl for Passion.com, but something in her eyes told me all was not fun and games in her world. She trembled a little, and her frequent side glances at the front door told me she might be frightened.

She wore a sleeveless turquoise V-necked blouse, black slacks, and open-toed black pumps. I couldn't see the heels beneath the slacks, but whatever height they were made her about five-eleven. A glittering silver necklace adorned her swanlike neck. She wore a silver bracelet on each slender wrist, a gold watch and two sparkling silver rings on each hand. Her thick golden hair was brushed back and hung loose, with long tendrils dangling near her cheeks. It had obviously cost her a bundle to get her hair looking that way. In my humble opinion, it was worth every penny.

Like all guys with healthy, active hormones, I wondered how she looked naked. I realized how sexist that sounded but I just couldn't help it. This woman had everything a man could ask for—flawless looks, slimness, lots of hair, extremely long legs, a soft, low voice…

She even smelled good. Despite my urge to cling to the devil-may-care attitude, I quickly found that, for me, the most difficult thing right now was to keep my drooling down to the bare minimum.

She obviously belonged to someone with money. What I couldn't figure out was why she was sitting over there all alone. Nor could I decide why in heaven's name she'd just approached me.

I got up from my stool and struggled not to act like an idiot. Believe me, this was much harder than it sounded. As much as I wanted to act dignified and reserved, I found that this woman was making me feel just as awkward and as stupid as I'd felt in high school when I'd found myself in the same room as the Homecoming Queen.

"Can I help you?" I was surprised that my voice actually worked. I was also surprised that I wasn't drooling.

"I…don't know how to ask you this…" She lowered her head and stared at the floor. I expected her to put her palms together and pray but realized how stupid that sounded.

A moment later, I followed suit, gazing stupidly at her painted toenails before snapping out of it and shifting my attention to the floor. It was ceramic tile, copper in color. Although the squares were all different, it was hard to notice that in the dim bar lighting. But no one went to a bar that was well-lit, and certainly no one went to a bar to examine the floor.

If Mike had been here, she would have told me that I was staring at the floor and looked ridiculous.

I imagined that I did indeed look ridiculous, as well as stupid. This was all it took to snap me out of it. I straightened. Then I wrenched myself out of my sex fantasy and decided to find out exactly what this lady wanted. "Just ask away," I told her.

Those big blue eyes began searching mine. "I was just wondering. Could you...I mean, would you mind very much if...if you went outside with me and walked me to my car?"

It sounded like an innocent request, but in my line of work, nothing that sounds innocent actually is. "I wouldn't mind at all. Might I ask why?"

She took a breath. Her voice was very soft, almost inaudible over the classic Chicago number, "*Make Me Smile*," thumping through the wall speakers when she said, "Someone's following me."

***

A popular fantasy of the average private detective—as well as a top-notch one, such as myself—involves a beautiful blonde sashaying into his office and offering him a lot of money to find the badass who's been making her life miserable.

The blonde is always tall and slender, always sexy and mysterious, with a soft, husky voice as well as an urgent breathless quality about her and the strong hint of sex following her around like a cheap perfume.

That had been my fantasy for some time, and although I'd been in the sleuthing business for many years, I'd reached the conclusion long ago that this silly dream was merely a holdover from my days as a horny adolescent and would never come to pass.

However, I'd learned long ago that to assume anything in this life was the sign of an idiot, and when I encountered the blond goddess in Sheffield's Bar, I realized right off that my longtime observation—like most other things I'd learned as a young adult—had been totally wrong.

I could tell right then that this babe might be in serious trouble. The way she trembled and the fear in her big blue eyes told me her request was not just a ruse to get picked up. The room was filled with other likely prospects she might have picked long before I'd even walked in. But for some strange reason, she'd chosen me. And this was what aroused my suspicions most of all.

Even so, the professional in me took over right away, shoving the horny, drool-prone adolescent aside and assessing the situation as it first appeared. It told me that I needed to ask her a few questions before deciding what to do.

"Why would someone be following you?"

"I honestly don't know. He could be a friend of my ex-husband's, for all I know."

"So we're talking about a he?"

"I think so…"

"You haven't actually seen anyone?"

"I noticed a car close behind me, so I decided to stop here and see if it turned off. If I was right, I didn't want anyone following me home."

That was definitely a good move on her part.

"Did it turn off?"

She shook her head.

I scanned the dark room. There were dozens of guys sitting at tables, but aside from the few lecherous glances this girl had earned for obvious reasons, I saw nothing suspicious. "Do you know if anyone came in here right after you?"

A nod. "I watched the front window when I first came inside. After a few minutes, I saw a man get out of a car and come in."

"Is this when you went over to the bar and ordered a drink?"

If you think you're being followed, stopping at a bar and having a drink isn't exactly the most sensible move you can make.

"When I saw him coming in, I went down the hall, opened the door to the ladies' room and slipped halfway inside, but kept an eye out in the hall. From where I was, I could see him come in."

"What did he look like?"

"I didn't get a good look at him. I guess he could have been about your height, maybe a little broader…"

"You didn't see his face?"

"He was too far away and wasn't standing near the light. And he was wearing a baseball cap pulled down low. I think it might have been a Gators cap. I'm not sure."

"What happened after that?"

"I waited to see if he'd come down the hall, but he didn't. I waited a couple of minutes. Then I saw him walk right back outside."

"Is his car still out there?"

"Until about twenty minutes ago. I thought I'd just wait him out and hope he'd get tired of all this and drive away."

"What kind of car was he driving?"

"It looked like a muscle car. A Camaro, or maybe a Challenger. Or Charger. All those cars look alike to me."

"Was it light or dark-colored?"

"It looked black, but you can't really tell in the dark. He didn't park under a streetlamp or anywhere near one."

This alone told me that if she was right, the man following her didn't clearly want to be seen. "Want me to take a stroll out there and check it out for you?"

She sighed. "Could you?"

I shrugged. "I could, just to be safe…"

"What if he's out there somewhere?"

"Then we'll take it from there."

She lowered her head and went back to watching the floor again. "I really appreciate this."

"Just give me a minute. I'll be right back."

I left a five-spot on the counter and went outside. Then I went out onto the front stoop and scanned the lot.

A light-colored Camaro was parked in the row facing the building, but no one was in it. Most of the other vehicles were pickups, although a BMW and a couple of compacts sat in the center of the aisle. A light-colored Lexus sat by itself at the far end. On the other side of it, a long row of thick bushes running parallel to a wooden fence separated the lot from the restaurant next door.

As far as I knew, her story could go either way. The professional in me wanted to believe it was just a story, but the man in me remembered the trembling and the wide-eyed look and wanted to think she was telling the truth. But since I didn't see anything suspicious, I knew I had nothing else to do but go back inside and tell her nothing looked out of the ordinary. If she were truly scared and convinced she was being followed, she'd be grateful the threat was over. And unless I was mistaken, gratefulness in a frightened woman often led to a night of unbridled lust and passion.

My goddess was sitting on her stool at the bar when I went back inside.

I walked over to her. "No one out there sitting in a dark Camaro, Challenger or Charger. You're good to go."

She sighed in relief. "I'm really grateful for you doing that. Thank you *so* much..."

"You're welcome."

She got up. "Could I ask you just one last tiny favor?"

"What is it?"

"Walk me to my car?"

"No problem."

She opened her clutch and pulled out a thick wad. I was obviously right about her having money. She peeled off a twenty, dropped it on the counter and slipped past me so close that her hip brushed against me. I felt a slight shudder.

"You okay?" I asked.

She smiled. The faintest trace of a dimple appeared near the left corner of her mouth. "Now I

18

am," she whispered, her minty breath lighting up a fire low in my gut.

Soon we were outside, walking down the long aisle of cars, until we came to the one at the very end, about five spaces from the last vehicle. It was the light-colored Lexus.

"Why so far away?" I asked.

"It was the first one I could find. When I got here, the place was more crowded. Besides, I was really frightened and didn't know where else to go. I wasn't thinking very clearly."

Her Lexus had extremely dark tint in the windows and a wax job that made it sparkle in the dark, even though the closet streetlamp was fifty feet away. Pricey. For a girl like her, I figured as much.

"Like I said, you're good to go."

"Thank you again." She showed me that tiny dimple once again and held out her hand. Then, just as I took it, she moved closer and planted a warm kiss on my lips. Before I could respond, she pulled away. "Maybe we could see one another again sometime soon?"

"Sure," I said, trying to keep my hormones from embarrassing me. "What's your name?"

"Sara Rhodes."

"I'm Ralph Deacon."

"I really do have to go. Thanks again. I mean it. We do need to get together and have a few drinks."

"When?"

"How about tomorrow night? Here? At six? Then we can have dinner. You pick the place. And after dinner, who knows?" She was staring at my mouth.

"Sounds great."

"Bye, Ralph. And thanks again."

"Good night." I turned and began walking across the lot. My pride and joy, the '75 black TransAm, awaited me near the short wooden fence neighboring the property line on the opposite side of the lot. Just when I was about halfway back to the car, the loud penetrating sound of a car alarm shattered the night air.

I spun around. The alarm was coming from the Lexus.

"What's going on?" Mike had suddenly appeared beside me.

"What?" I could hardly hear her over the ear-splitting racket.

She moved closer. "I said, what's happening?"

"I honestly don't know."

"What did you do?"

"Nothing."

"You didn't set off that alarm?"

"I didn't touch the car at all." I took a few steps closer. When I was about ten feet from the Lexus, I reached out for the driver's door to see what had happened.

"I wouldn't get any closer if I were you," Mike cautioned.

"I've got to find out what's going on. The car hasn't budged." I took another step.

"Do you trust me?" Mike looked grim.

"Of course." My pulse was racing. A woman I'd just talked to could be in serious trouble. "I've got to find out if she's—"

"Trust me and don't move. At all."

The professional in me finally took over and told me that until I found out what just happened, I didn't need to put my hands anywhere near that Lexus.

"Do me a favor," I told Mike. "Take a look inside."

She slipped inside the vehicle. Moments later, she reappeared beside me. Her expression was grim.

I was afraid to ask. "Is she in there?"

"I see a blond woman."

"What's she doing?"

"Not much. She's dead."

"What?"

"She's slouched in the back seat of the Lexus."

"You sure she's dead?"

"Her throat's been cut. There's blood all over the seat and on the floor."

"Were you able to see her? Her spirit? I mean, when she—"

"She was already gone by the time I saw her."

"Nothing about what happened?"

Mike shook her head. "Sorry. She obviously left her body long before now."

Just then, two police cars pulled into the lot, their lights flashing. They stopped about twenty feet away. Their passenger doors flung open. Two cops jumped out and stood close to their doors for protection. Their guns were pointed directly at me.

"Freeze!" one of them yelled.

Chapter 3

"That's it?"

Judging by his curt reaction, Neil apparently didn't believe my incredible tale.

"That was the whole story."

He ran a big-knuckled hand over his rust-colored brush cut. "Let me get this straight. You went to Sheffield's on East Colonial for a drink. Then this statuesque blonde approached you and told you someone was following her. This same babe asked you to walk her back to her car. And once you turned around to head back to your own car, a car alarm went off right behind you. It was the car alarm in the babe's Lexus, and when you went back to it, OPD showed up and told you to freeze. And when you did, they walked over, opened the door of the Lexus and saw her lying in the back seat with her throat slit open?"

"That's what happened."

He thought about that a few moments and confusion instantly covered his face. "You didn't see anyone else hiding or moving around near the Lexus?"

"Nope."

"And you said you couldn't see inside the vehicle?"

"The tint was pretty dark." Since Mike had seen her and I hadn't, I knew to tread lightly. "I only saw her when OPD opened the door."

"And you couldn't see her at all before this?"

"Nope."

"Makes sense." He blinked. "You couldn't possibly have seen anything in that car unless you stuck your face against the window."

"I wasn't really sure about anything. Good thing your guys showed when they did." I shrugged.

"And you're one hundred percent positive you didn't touch anything?"

"I was tempted to. Hell, I wanted to open the door and see what happened, but by the time the shock wore off, OPD had already got there and told me not to move."

"Good thing you did as they said. It's your one and only get-out-of-jail-free card."

"Did they tell you anything about the nine-one-one call?"

"I haven't heard much about anything yet. I got here as soon as they told me what happened. They did say the call was anonymous, so this tells me it's already suspect."

"Did a man or woman call it in?"

Neil fished his cell out of his pocket and asked for the officer assigned to the case. Then he got up and began walking up and down the dimly lit little room, mumbling occasionally. Two minutes later, he shut the cell and pocketed it. "They said the caller's voice was raspy. They're not even sure if it was a man or woman, but they're working on it to get a voice print."

"Terrific."

Neil watched me for a few moments. "You said there were others at the bar."

"I figure around twenty or so."

"Any of 'em other men?"

23

"It was kind of dark, but yeah, I'd say most of them were guys. Sheffield's is a pickup bar."

"And this gorgeous blonde picked you?"

I shrugged.

Neil scratched his jaw. "Out of all the guys in that room, this beautiful blonde picked you to escort her back to her car?"

"You're beginning to sound insulting, Neil."

"He might actually have a point," Mike said, appearing on my cot on my left.

"I know," I whispered without thinking.

"Howzat?"

"Just thinking out loud."

"I can't leave you for a second, can I?" she asked.

I just shrugged.

"I don't know about all this, Deacon." Neil rubbed his temples.

"I didn't kill her, Neil."

"I know."

"Any way I can get out of here?"

He stopped pacing and looked pensive for a moment. "I'll see what I can do."

"I don't know how much I can come up with, bail-wise."

"Well, if your DNA isn't on the victim or anywhere in or on the Lexus, you won't be considered a perp, so you won't even need bail." He went over to the cell door. While the guard was unlocking it, Neil turned and said, "Give me an hour. I'll make some calls."

"Thanks for coming in to save my ass."

He mumbled something inaudible as he turned and disappeared down the hall.

"Why is he like that?" Mike asked.

I didn't say anything. I just pointed kind of subtly at the little black box above the door.

Mike nodded. "I understand. I guess we can just sit here and enjoy one another's company."

I shrugged, lowered my head and whispered, "I'm glad you're here."

"Want me to go see what he's doing?"

"It's all right." I was talking into my hands. "Neil knows his job. He'll come through for me."

Mike nodded. "Okay, then. We'll just sit quietly until I run out of ectoplasm again and fade off into the sunset. Sound good to you?"

I nodded.

***

As I'd suspected, Neil knew exactly who to talk to about this.

Less than an hour after he'd left, the guard opened my cell door and told me I was free to leave.

At the desk, the sergeant gave me back my wallet, car keys, watch, and my .380 Cheetah, which they'd found in the glovebox of my TransAm. I checked everything, pocketed it and signed for it. "Any idea where I can find my car?"

He shrugged a shoulder and tried hard not to look bored. "It's out back in the lot."

"Not in Impound?"

He shook his head.

"I wonder how that happened."

He gave me a sour look. Obviously not in the mood for an in-depth discussion. These guys were

25

generally not very chatty. "You wanna complain, you need to take it somewhere else."

"I'm not complaining, believe me."

He just shrugged and went back to his crossword puzzle.

The TransAm was where he'd said it was, at the far end of the second aisle in the rear lot, facing the building. I didn't see any scratches or signs of negligence, and there were no scuff marks on the tires.

"How about this white smudge on the roof?" Mike asked, drifting over.

"Bird shit."

"Lovely." She drifted toward the back. "There's another one on the rear bumper."

"I like to park near trees. You know that."

"So do the birds, apparently."

Satisfied, I opened the driver door. The seat had been pulled back to accommodate a much larger individual. Other than that, my treasured classic ride appeared unmolested. The gas gauge was only about a quarter of an inch closer to empty, telling me the big guy bringing it here hadn't decided to have some fun and take it on I-4 to hear how it sounded when it was opened up.

So far, life was approaching the tolerant level again.

I got back to my one-bedroom South Conway condo shortly before one that morning.

As usual, the guard sitting on his stool in the tiny metal shack fifty feet inside the condominium entrance was fast asleep.

I sighed in relief. I was exhausted and in no mood to answer any more questions. When he was awake, the old guy irritated everyone with mindless chitchat. He was obviously lonely and bored—which translated into instant exasperation for whoever he stopped before they could slip past.

However, just as I approached the little building, he snapped awake and nearly fell off his stool staggering outside. "Wait!"

Cursing softly, I slammed on the brakes.

"I don't see why you treat this poor man so badly," Mike said, sitting beside me. "He seems to like you."

"He doesn't even know me."

"Then why does he always stop you and talk to you?"

"He does this to everyone."

"But he really seems to enjoy doing it with you."

"Maybe it's my irresistible charm."

"I thought that only worked on women…"

"I wish it did."

The old guy, pushing eighty, moved in slow motion, with a pronounced limp. An old war injury, he'd once told me. Since his limp changed from one leg to the other from time to time, I somehow found myself figuring arthritis more than shrapnel or a bullet wound. But anything was possible.

He shuffled over and bent. Then, squinting behind his small round specs, he said, "You okay? Look sorta…well, spooked."

I didn't want to tell him I was with a woman just a few seconds before her throat was cut and had been arrested because of it. The old guy knew I was a detective and had been living here for several years. He'd seen me when I was beat up and had been here when a couple of shady characters had broken into my apartment.

He was also a blabbermouth. I didn't want him talking to the Association again. They didn't like me or the trouble I'd brought with me from time to time. They were looking for any excuse they could find that would enable them to get me to leave. My lifestyle was too violent for them. Many of the people living in the complex were retired and elderly. Violence was the last thing they wanted to see on the property.

But I liked my place and its location. I didn't want to scare him, so I said, "I was almost in an accident."

He blinked and dropped his jaw. "Really? Where?"

"The road."

"Where exactly?"

"Just down from the Mall."

"Which one?"

I sighed deeply. I should have figured that since he'd just had his nap, he'd be fresh and rested up, and ready to be chatty and inquisitive. However, I'd just escaped death and a night in jail. I wanted to get home, lie down and sleep. "The one with all the traffic."

While he was thinking that one over, I waved and hurried away.

"You should have told that poor man what happened," Mike said.

"Why?"

"He wanted to know."

"I'd be sitting back there for the next hour, dammit. I'm much too tired and shaken up."

"He seems nice."

"He's just bored and wants an audience."

"You're very cynical, you know."

"A cynical private eye? Fancy that."

She frowned. "You're really get cranky when you're tired."

"Could it possibly be because I was with a woman who had her throat cut just thirty seconds after I walked away from her? And just as I was about to grasp what happened, I was arrested, tossed in a squad car and carted off to the Police Station?"

"Sure. Let's go with that."

"Imagine that. Maybe I actually have feelings."

Mike smiled. "I love it when you open up…"

"I love it when you understand me," I said flatly.

"That didn't sound very sincere."

"Possibly because I'm so damned cynical."

Mike just sighed.

I parked in my designated spot, got out, crossed the dark, deserted street and went up the short grassy knoll leading to my condo.

After a strong drink, I peeled my half-dead body out of my clothes, collapsed in my bed and did not move.

Chapter 4

Neil looked just as unkempt and irritable as he watched me walk into his office at the Police Station that same morning.

His tiny blue eyes were bloodshot and a little glazed, his uniform more wrinkled than usual as he handed me a cup of boiling black coffee. He'd obviously changed in his office but had done it quickly. The two undone buttons on his shirt suggested that his heart hadn't really been in it.

I placed the cup very gently on the edge of the metal desk top. Then I sat in the chair facing his desk and stared at the deadly concoction slowly melting the Styrofoam cup as the fumes formed a thick gray cloud bubbling up. I'd had coffee with my breakfast half an hour earlier and didn't need any for a while. Good thing. The smell of Neil's brew was revolting. It was also so hot that it singed my eyebrows the moment he'd handed me the cup even though I was careful to hold it away from my face. Neil was a great cop; he just had no idea how to make coffee without turning it into a corrosive acid that could melt flesh right off the bone.

Neil sat down and glared at me. I could tell it wasn't one of his "angry" glares. This was the kind that showed when he was confused or frustrated. Neil didn't like it much when he tried wrapping his head around something that made no sense to him. But he'd never been one to let a mystery linger, and always got right to the point.

Neil grabbed his cup and had some coffee. He grimaced as he set it back down but didn't double up, faint or begin to gasp. This told me he was used to it, and it no longer bothered him. I couldn't imagine this being a good thing.

"Thanks for getting me out," I told him.

"Just don't be a butthole and let me find out you actually killed that woman."

"Be real. When was the last time I killed a woman?"

He shrugged. "I have no idea. You never told me you ever did."

"There's a good reason for that."

"I know, I know." He pushed his two brows together and looked like he was smelling something foul.

"What's wrong?" I asked. I knew Neil pretty well. When he looked like that and didn't say anything, something was bothering him.

"I know what you told me last night…"

"And?"

"To be blunt, I don't like it at all."

"Like what?"

"Most of it. All of it, actually."

"Let me repeat myself. Like what?"

"Take a piece of it—any piece—and toss it over here."

"All right. How about her picking me out?"

"That's a good start."

I didn't reply. My ego had already begun chafing a little, but my professional nose had already taken over. Despite my bruised ego, something about this made no sense.

31

Neil opened the folder on his desk. "Report says the Lexus was parked at the far end of the front lot, a good thirty feet from the nearest vehicle."

"She said she couldn't park any closer. When she first got there, the front lot was nearly filled."

"That's something else we won't know until we interview the owners of the bar."

"I just hope they can help. It's hard watching the front lot when you're in the office in back or tending bar."

"Something else I can't get my little mind around."

"Keep going."

"You didn't hear anything touch the Lexus before the alarm went off?"

"No."

"Then we're talking remote."

"Maybe."

"You know what that means, right?"

"Conspiracy?"

"Very possible. Besides, I don't like the alternative."

"Her killer was waiting for her in the Lexus?"

"This would mean he slit her throat the second she climbed in and took less than two seconds to do it."

"How'd he get her in the back seat first?"

"That's another major clinker. Possibly even bigger than the tiny time element."

"Actually, I think both details are equally fantastic."

32

Neil nodded. "So, our killer pulls her into the back seat, slits her throat, slips out of the Lexus and triggers the alarm, all in what? Twenty seconds?"

"I don't think it took that long, actually."

"Then what are we talking? Ten? Fifteen?"

"The amount of time it took me to turn around and take about ten, maybe twelve steps."

Neil shook his head.

"I know. Doesn't make sense, does it?"

"Especially since you didn't see anyone slipping out of the Lexus and hightailing it. Do you remember hearing the car door opening? Slamming shut?"

"No…"

"You're sure?"

The more I thought of it, the more I realized I didn't hear anything but the traffic buzzing down Colonial. "Positive."

"That makes it a *little* easier, then…"

"They didn't find any blood on the pavement on the other side of the Lexus?"

"None."

"This means the killer's either the most efficient in the world or that he knows exactly how to keep away from the spray."

"Not likely in either case. Especially since her killer didn't use a car door to leave."

"Then you know what that means, right?"

He nodded. "It means no one got out of the Lexus."

"So how did she get her throat slit?"

"The usual way. The killer, on the other hand, is another story."

"Did you guys have time to print the knife yet?"

"No prints. Both blade and handle were wiped clean. The only thing on it was her blood."

"This is really screwy."

Neil had another sip of battery acid.

"What are you thinking?" I asked.

He put the cup down and stared at it. "I just can't wrap my mind around someone following her and slipping into her car, then pulling her into the back seat and slitting her throat when she comes back out with you. Then disappearing, and without using the door to get out of the car."

"It does sound like some sort of a bad dream, doesn't it?"

"I'm just not totally convinced that murder was all it was cracked up to be."

"We don't exactly have much to work with, do we?"

"It would have been much better for all of us if you'd touched the Lexus, or opened the door and handled the knife…"

"Much better for who?"

"Touché. I'd even like it a lot more if you'd turned around to watch her get back into the Lexus."

"Now what fun would that be?"

Neil went back to studying the report again. He picked up his cup and sipped more coffee. "Even if whoever did her jimmied his way into the Lexus, waited for her in the back seat, pulled her back with him, slit her throat, then snuck back out like a ghost, how the hell'd he get away in all that traffic?"

"He could have had the getaway car parked next door, at the seafood restaurant."

"And since OPD was concentrating on Sheffield's, they wouldn't have noticed traffic in any of the other lots."

"All he had to do was get into his car and pull out. He was probably driving by the same time your guys showed and started pointing guns at me."

Neil was shaking his head again. "This still doesn't explain how he got out of that car without you or anyone else seeing or hearing him. Especially you, since you were just twenty or thirty feet away, and there was no other vehicle parked on the other side of the Lexus."

"All I saw were some bushes on the other side of the Lexus."

Nodded shrugged. "That would definitely conceal someone crawling past."

"I really feel bad about all this."

"Why?"

"She told me she was being followed. I went outside and had a look around to make sure no one was being suspicious. Then I let her get back in her car. Now she's dead."

"You didn't know what was going on."

"So?"

"You still don't."

"So?"

"Would you have done things differently if you had?"

"Damned straight."

"Then get off the self-pity. You have no idea what this woman was into."

35

He was right, but it still didn't make me feel any better.

Neil went pensive again. "Something else about this is bugging me."

"What?"

"No matter what she said about it being crowded, she coulda parked closer to the door."

"But she said—"

"The place has handicapped spaces."

"She's not—she wasn't—handicapped."

"If she was as scared as she'd let on, she woulda said hell and risked getting a ticket. She would have just parked as close to the front door as possible."

"I guess you've got a point there…"

"You sound doubtful."

"Right now, I'm kind of doubtful about everything. But where are you going with this?"

"Put this one in your head and toss it around. How many women who think they're being followed would waste time parking a hundred feet from the front entrance of a building when there are not two, but *three* handicapped spaces right outside the door?"

***

Neil's phone buzzed just as I was about to leave.

He picked it up. He immediately frowned, glanced at me, and sighed. I could tell something bad was about to happen. "Send 'em both in." He put down the phone and stared at it for a moment. I could tell right off that my guess had been right. He straightened and gave me one of his grim looks.

36

"The two detectives assigned to the case. They're here."

Knowing Neil as well as I did, I tried a gamble. "I guess you want me to behave?"

Neil blinked. "Have you forgotten what happened to you last night?"

"You mean when I went to Sheffield's?"

"After that."

"The woman lying in the Lexus with her throat cut?"

"Just a little past that."

"I was arrested."

He slapped the desk blotter with his palm. "I knew you'd get it. Eventually."

"How could I forget something like that? First of all, accommodations were awful, and no food was provided."

"If you'd stayed a little longer, we might have had enough time to get our act together to make your stay comfier…"

"That's all right. I just wasn't in the mood to stay there. Things to do, right?"

"What I'm trying to say is—"

"Stay off the case?"

Neil frowned. "Will ya stay out of it if I tell ya to?"

"Let me think about that for a moment. Probably not."

He nodded. Neil knew me just as well as I knew him. "All right, then. Just remember this. These two are on the job. If I know cops, they'll still consider you the prime suspect. In other words, the best thing you can do is stay the hell out of their way, all right?"

"No problem."

He continued glaring. I could tell he didn't trust me. "I mean it, Deacon. I might not be able to smooth things over if ya get in their way and start stepping on toes."

"I'll tread lightly."

The door opened.

Two large men dressed in dark suits came in. Neil introduced them as Detective Harry Davenport and Lou Gaffman. Davenport was big, about six-three, and went at least two-forty. Gaffman, smaller at around six feet, was solid and probably tipped the scales at one-ninety. They both scowled at me when they came in and stood next to the door, watching Neil.

Neil introduced us.

"Why isn't he in a cell, Chief?" Davenport said, glaring at me.

I wanted to tell him that I didn't like my cell and preferred sleeping in my own bed, but I knew that wouldn't go over very well. Davenport was obviously the type who didn't put up with smartassed remarks. Besides, my gut was telling me to keep quiet or I'd regret it. And I didn't want to upset Neil. He'd already stuck his neck out for me.

"He's not a suspect," Neil replied flatly.

Gaffman shrugged. "We were told—"

"I honestly don't care what you were told. The lack of DNA evidence already cleared him."

"I still think he oughta be—"

"It's nice that you still think," Neil said. His cold stare did a number on Gaffman, who took a step back and glanced at the door.

"No offense, Chief," Davenport said, still glaring at me, "but we don't need a private dick gettin' in our way with this. Especially when he was the prime suspect."

"He's actually the prime eyewitness," Neil said. "There's a difference."

I knew better than jump in and add anything. When two stallions were fighting, the most dangerous and stupid thing in the world was to get in between them. Besides, I knew my place. Cops didn't approve of private detectives. One reason was that sometimes the less experienced of us actually did get in their way. Another was that they knew it looked bad for them if the detective managed to solve the case before they could. I preferred to consider their dislike for me as a jealousy sort of thing. Plus the fact that they obviously thought I'd slit the woman's throat.

"You might want his help," Neil said firmly.

"I'm still surprised he's not a suspect." Davenport couldn't stop glaring at me. "From what we heard, he was right there at the murder scene."

"He's not stupid, ya know."

"That's not what *I* heard."

I had to struggle to refrain from telling Davenport that he obviously needed an explosive bowel movement to release the pressure in his brain. But I knew better than state the obvious.

"Regardless of what you might have heard, he's not stupid. Only an idiot would slit a woman's throat, get out of the damned car and just stand there like an idiot instead of running."

"Maybe he didn't have enough time to make tracks.

"Enough," Neil snapped. "The man didn't do it. Besides, I've already vouched for him."

Davenport was silent for a few moments. Even so, both Neil and I could tell he was fuming. I was even certain I could hear his sphincter puckering. Maybe he actually *would* have a bowel movement soon. He finally took a breath and said, "Even if he's no longer a suspect, he still needs to stay out of this. We might find some clues later on that proves he's our man. Then where do we stand?"

Gaffman didn't say anything, but I had the distinct impression he didn't want to get involved in all this sparring. He looked like a man who was trying his best to fade away.

"I should think that a suspect would have left some sort of clue in this case," Neil said. "Wouldn't you?"

Before either could answer, Neil added, "I'd like either of you to tell me how anyone could slit someone's throat open in a confined space and get away without leaving one drop of blood—or even a single print—in evidence."

Davenport opened his mouth to protest, but Neil beat him to the punch. "Impossible, wouldn't you say?"

Davenport's mouth stayed open, but nothing came out.

"I knew you'd understand." Neil flashed a quick smile that instantly died. "So, before you both let yourselves get all worked up over this and develop an ulcer or a bad case of nerves, lemme tell ya something. This man has a better track record of anyone I've ever seen. He's got a nose for clues and knows how to put things together even when there's very little—or even nothing—to go on. So, to repeat myself, you just might want his help."

Davenport's glaring eyes suggested that he hadn't liked what Neil had said. Whatever he saw on Neil's face had apparently convinced him not to protest.

Neil turned to me. "As I told ya just a few minutes ago, these detectives are working this case. If I were you, I'd let them do their job."

Davenport grunted.

"If you prefer," Neil said in a somewhat softer tone, "I'll be the middleman here. If Deacon manages to stumble onto something, he calls me. If I think it's pertinent, I'll call you two and tell you what he found. How's that?"

Just as Davenport opened his mouth, Neil said, "I'm glad you boys agree." Neil turned to me. "Get that, Deacon? Ya find something? Call me right away and I'll relay it to these two fine detectives."

"Terrific. Peachy keen."

"Great. Just so we're all on the same page, then…" Neil picked up his Styrofoam cup. The two of us watched as the detectives stormed out of the room and slammed the door.

"Thanks, Neil."

He took a sip, put down the cup and belched. Then he glared at me. "Don't let me down, Deacon."

41

"I won't."

"I know ya won't."

"I'll probably end up solving this case."

"I know ya will."

"Then why the nasty face?"

"I know you're good and I know you'll get this solved long before they will. But you're a smartass, and with those two, it'll cost ya."

"I told you I'll tread lightly."

"Do what you gotta do. Find whoever did this. Just do it quietly and as tactfully as you can, without getting those two pissed. And be careful, all right?"

Chapter 5

I drove back to Sheffield's on East Colonial and parked in the front lot of the seafood place next door so I could have a good view of the crime scene.

Before getting out, I sat behind the wheel, staring at the place while I went over what Neil and I had discussed in his office.

Sheffield's provided three handicapped spots located almost directly in front of the entrance. However, instead of zipping into one of them and scurrying inside, my blond goddess chose to park in the farthest spot, half a dozen spaces from the nearest vehicle.

"What are you thinking?" Mike asked, appearing in the seat beside me.

"What if all three handicapped spots were occupied when she got here?"

"That would mean she couldn't have parked there, then…"

Mike was right. So why didn't this convince me?

"You know the chances of those three spots being taken all at once are pretty slim, don't you?" she asked.

"That's what's bugging me."

"When you came outside with her last night, were they empty?"

"All three of them?"

"Yes."

43

I tried remembering. I wasn't sure, but I didn't recall any vehicles parked close to the front door. "I don't think so."

"Are you sure?"

"Not positive, but reasonably certain."

"There you have it, then."

I thought about that for a moment. "But that doesn't mean they were vacant when she first got there, does it?"

"No…"

"This takes us back to square one."

"Exactly."

Frustrated, I got out. Then, stepping over the short wooden fence separating the lots and squeezing between the bushes, I went over to the front of the building.

"What do you expect to find?" Mike asked.

"I have no idea."

"Why did we come back, then?"

"I'm looking for something to tell me what happened, I guess. Something I hadn't thought of yet. Something I might have missed." I moved closer to the handicapped spots. I didn't know what I was looking for—an oil spot, a crumpled cigarette—but I found myself staring, nonetheless.

"There's nothing there."

"I know."

"I guess I'm trying to tell you that this might be a waste of time."

"I know that, too."

"Then why are we still here?"

"As I just said, I'm trying to figure out what happened."

"You know what happened."

"I was right here. I could have been murdered with her."

Mike shook her head. "I think you're looking at this all wrong."

"How should I be looking at it?"

"You should be asking yourself the same things your rude police buddy was asking."

"You really need to give Neil a break. After all, he got me out of jail, you know. And he stood up for me when Davenport wanted to roast me over the coals."

"I know. He's still rude."

"Maybe, but—"

"No maybes."

"Now you've made me forget what we were talking about."

"Why she parked where she parked."

"I'm trying really hard to figure out why she parked way the hell over there, rather than right in front of the door."

"You need to ask yourself different questions."

"Like what?"

"For instance, why did she pick you out of all those other guys in the room?"

I shrugged. "Neil said it was because I was alone."

"I think he was right. She was looking for someone the cops could blame for the murder. You were alone. It sounds very simple when we look at it that way."

"But why fabricate a story about being followed just to find someone you can use as a patsy for a murder?"

"To make her appear more convincing?"

"Could be..."

"She had to do it that way. She couldn't take any chances. After all, you don't look that stupid."

"Thanks, Mike."

"You asked, right?"

"Yeah. I asked." Just then, I turned back to the building.

"What do you see?" she asked.

"The blinds."

"What about them?"

"See how they're wide-open?"

"Customers can see out the windows right now... But at night?"

"Exactly."

"Exactly what?"

"Whoever slit that woman's throat knew that. They probably also knew that there's a corner booth facing that last window, where the Lexus was parked."

"Others could still see. That wall is lined with booths, right?"

"Right. But this tells me something very interesting."

"What's that?"

"For some reason we haven't quite figured out yet, the killer wasn't too worried about being seen."

***

My thoughts continued to loop as I climbed back into the TransAm and called Neil on my cell.

I didn't know exactly what to say to him but knew that since talking to Mike, I had a shitload of questions to ask that had just turned this case completely around.

"What is it, Deacon? I'm pretty busy right now."

"Did anything else come in about the dead girl?"

I heard him shifting papers. "Something did a few minutes ago. Girl was who she told you she was. Name was Sara Rhodes. Twenty-seven, part-time stripper at Vesper's."

"Any priors?"

"Small-time stuff. Prostitution a few years back, brought in a couple times on possession of marijuana, petty theft. But nothing big."

"She must have been pulling in some serious bucks stripping part-time to afford that Lexus. They go for fifty K, easy. Was it hers? Or stolen?"

"She'd bought it two months ago. Car was registered in her name. VIN number matches. Nothing different about the murder. She was found in the back seat, but the blood spatter was inconsistent with the appearance of the murder."

"How so?"

"Lab thinks she was unconscious when her throat was cut. They also think the spatter was controlled so the killer didn't get any of the blood on him. Or her."

"How about the act itself?"

"Simple and direct. The killer was behind her, possibly on the right side of the car. The job was done by pulling her by the hair and slicing her, left to right."

"Most of the blood spatter hit the passenger seat in the back, then?"

"Right. Neat job if you look at it from that standpoint."

"So...whoever did it used gloves and had their right arm protected from the blood spatter?"

"Correct."

"This would mean the girl was probably put into the back unconscious, her face pointed toward the floor."

"It also means that whoever did it is a psycho and needs to be caught. The blade was long and sharp. Nicked the cord. Lots of force behind it. It suggests rage—which also tells us it was personal."

"Did the girl have a twin?"

"Not that we know of."

"You're sure?"

"Nothing turned up."

"I knew that would be much too easy."

"Why bring it up, then?"

"I'm still trying to figure out where she went."

"You were there. You tell me."

"I'm wondering if the killer had a partner."

"I guess that's something we need to figure out if we wanna close the case, isn't it?"

"Well, whoever did this did a bang-up job."

"It was well-planned. That much we know."

"Damned straight. The killer murdered a woman, left her in the back seat of her own car in a crowded parking lot, and made tracks with one of

Orlando's best private detectives standing around like a shithead."

"Was there a detective out there with you? I thought you said you were alone."

"Funny, Neil." Sometimes the man could be just as much of an asshole as I was.

"Seriously, though, as I just told you, whoever did this is a psycho."

I didn't reply. Something off-the-wall was jumping around in my brain again.

"Deacon? Still there?"

"Yeah…"

"Let's have it. I can practically hear the gears grinding in that noggin."

"I'm getting the idea that you're not too concerned about this one."

"Well, so far, Davenport and Gaffman think it could be some sort of drug burn or a personal beef involving Vesper's. Since you're the only eyewitness, it's gonna probably be a quick solve."

"I can definitely hear a *but* in there somewhere."

"Let me put it this way—unless the Lab guys come up with something else, we're gonna put this one to rest damn shortly. Too many other cases out there."

"What about the fact that we might be facing a psycho?"

"We'll find him. Or her. You know it looks like this Rhodes babe was into something bad. She probably screwed the wrong guy. She was most likely done in by the poor sap she screwed. Maybe this sap paid someone to follow her and do her in.

Or maybe whoever did her used a decoy to get a patsy in there to make the deed look simple."

"So this other babe picked me because I was easy?"

"Could be. So, Rhodes gets her due and you're standing around with your thumb up your ass while the actual killer gets away."

"They really got away pretty damned fast."

"It was obviously well-planned. The woman with you just waited until your back was turned. Maybe she waited until you took two steps. Or maybe three. Let's say three, just to make sure you didn't turn around. The nine-one-one call had already been made, so that was already in the works. Then she circled the Lexus, got down low on the other side of the bushes, tapped the Lexus on her way into the next lot, and go away in another vehicle."

"She was wearing good clothes."

"Think that mattered?"

"Most women don't like getting their good clothes messed up."

"We're talking felony murder here."

"That might change her approach a tad, I guess…"

"But at least now we definitely know Rhodes was already dead long before you approached the Lexus."

"How about that? I'm innocent."

"Fancy that."

"And you didn't even need me this time. I'm hurt, Neil."

"Don't celebrate quite yet. There's still a lot of other stuff here. Prints have to be collected. Insurance claims and the lawsuits from the patrons who were detained have to be sorted through and processed. We're pretty sure what we have here is just another stripper babe who tried to screw the wrong guy. What we don't know is who did it. Like it or not, I kinda think you'll get this one nailed down faster than Davenport and Gaffman."

Neil was right. I didn't like it very much, but I couldn't argue with his analogy.

"Something else?" he asked.

"There's something very ironic about all this."

"You mean their picking the wrong patsy? The fact that anyone else would have instinctively tried to open the door when the alarm went off?"

"That's what I was thinking."

"If that had happened, this patsy would have had his prints all over everything and consequently would have framed himself for all this—which was most likely what this killer had planned."

"Yeah, good thing I didn't touch anything."

Once again, Mike had saved my bacon.

"One day you're gonna have to tell me about this ridiculous streak of good luck that's been following you around," Neil said. "I still haven't been able to figure out how you managed to sniff out that car bomb at the Florida Mall all those many years ago."

"That was just luck, I guess."

"You'll have to explain that one, too."

It was time to put this mystery to rest so he'd stop obsessing over it.

"Would you believe I was about to get into the TransAm when I dropped my keys? And that they hopped away from me and ended up underneath the chassis? And when I got down on my knees to reach for them, I saw this long, loose wire spanning from the gas tank to the battery?"

A long pause. "I guess that'll have to do."

"You sound unconvinced."

"That's probably 'cause I am. But unless something else comes at me, it'll have to do for now."

Sometimes Neil was impossible.

"Any other thoughts before I hang up and get back to more practical matters?"

"I don't think anything else from the crime scene will help," I said.

"To be blunt, this one's definitely grunt work. The big guns upstairs don't want us wasting a whole lotta man-hours on it. They're bean-counters, and I'm sure ya know they're looking to save money any which way they can."

I didn't reply.

"Sorry to burst your bubble."

"I guess I was right about the Rhodes babe all along."

"How d'ya mean?"

"A guy like me never runs into a gorgeous woman unless there's serious trouble following her around. Or unless she's already dead."

Chapter 6

After talking with Neil, I drove over to the Waffle House on Colonial to have lunch. The moment I sat down, my cell buzzed.

It was my mom.

"Hi, Mom. How are things in Lauderdale?" I tried to sound casual, but I could tell by the sound of her voice that something was on her mind.

"Just checking in."

"Really?" I knew for certain that something was up. "What's going on?"

"Do I have to have a reason for calling, Ralphie?"

She was obviously calling about something specific. "You usually have some ulterior motive, yes. And don't call me Ralphie."

"It's your name, honey. Your father and I—"

"I know what you named me, Mom. I go by Ralph these days. I've been going by Ralph for the last twenty years. I liked being called Ralph when I was in high school. But especially now. I *am* in my early forties, you know…"

"It doesn't matter. I'm your mother. You'll always be my little boy."

"Mom…" I wasn't exactly in the mood for this. I was hungry and wanted to eat. I was also a little unnerved about founding out that the woman I'd helped had been a prostitute and petty criminal, then put me in the middle of a murder that was looking more and more bizarre by the minute.

"Honestly, the way you treat your mother. If your father was still alive…"

"What's up, Mom?" I was growing more impatient by the second. The food smells drifting heavily from the kitchen were getting to me and I found myself salivating.

Just then, Mike appeared in the booth beside me.

A moment later, the skinny redheaded waitress came over and gave me a hint of tiny cleavage when she bent over my table and smiled. Her thick ponytail slid down her right shoulder and hung there, swaying. Needless to say, it distracted me even more than the food smells. "Ready to order?"

"I'd like a nice hot cup of coffee first off, if you don't mind."

"Coming right up…" She straightened, turned, flipped her ponytail over her shoulder and whisked away.

"Where are you, son?" Mom asked.

"Is that your rude policeman buddy?" Mike asked, gesturing to the phone.

"No, it's my mom."

"Who are you talking to, Ralphie?"

"My waitress, Mom—and don't call me Ralphie."

The redhead brought me over a cup of steaming black coffee and a small white carafe. She placed the cup in front of me and the carafe on my right. "Here ya go."

"Thank you."

"Where are you?" Mom asked.

"Waffle House."

54

"Why's your mom calling?" Mike asked.

"I think she's got something up her sleeve," I told Mike.

"Who's got something up her sleeve, Ralphie?"

"You do, Mom. And it's *Ralph*."

"Who are you talking to now, dear?"

"You."

"Besides me."

"My waitress."

"Have you decided what you'd like to have?" The redhead flicked her ponytail over her shoulder once again and got her pad ready to scribble on.

"I'd like a double cheeseburger and a large order of curly fries—"

"Ralphie, that sounds like too much fatty food."

"I can handle it, Mom. Besides, I'm hungry. It's been a rough morning."

"What did she say?" Mike asked.

"She says it's too much fatty food."

"Is it…all right?" The waitress looked concerned. Her large light-blue eyes gawked at me.

"It's just my mom. She thinks I'll collapse from a heart attack if I eat too much fatty food."

"She could be right, you know," Mike said.

"I'm Italian. I was raised on fatty food."

"That's right," Mike said. "I remember what they forced you to eat when we were down in Lauderdale for our visit."

"Dear, why are you talking to your waitress about the foods you ate as a child?"

"She asked."

"Are we good to go?" the waitress whispered uneasily.

55

I smiled at her and nodded.

She whisked away to get my order.

"You're not a kid anymore, Ralphie—"

"I know, Mom. And I feel just fine."

"You might feel just fine, Ralphie, but trust me, it sneaks up on you."

"As I just said, I'm having a rough day. I'll burn it off. And don't call me Ralphie."

"She just worries about you," Mike said. "After all, she *is* your mother, you know."

"I know."

"Just promise me you'll try and watch what you eat, honey. I know you're a little thin, but you've still got to pay attention to what you put in there—"

"Is this why you called, Mom? To pester me about my lunch?"

"I'm your mom, honey. I'm allowed to pester you. I'm calling about your Uncle Al. He's going into the hospital tomorrow morning."

"What's wrong with Uncle Al? He looked pretty good when I was down there last."

"That was two years ago, dear. And he is in his eighties, you know. But he's been having slight heart palpitations, so he decided to have himself checked out."

"He'll be okay, Mom. Don't worry. He's always been in good shape."

"I just thought I ought to call and let you know."

"Thanks. Tell him I said hi and hope everything turns out okay. How's Aunt Charlotte doing?"

"She's a little worried, but she'll be fine. You know her. She'll clean the house a couple of times and watch her soaps just to stay busy."

"What's wrong with Uncle Al?" Mike asked.

"He's having himself checked out tomorrow for palpitations."

"Oh, dear…"

"He's the sweet one, right? The short gentlemen with the dimples and the soft voice?"

"That's him."

"Ralphie, why are you talking to your waitress about your uncle?"

I took a breath and tried to stay in control, but my mom was getting on my last nerve. "I'm not talking to my waitress, Mom—and don't call me Ralphie."

"Who are you talking to, then?"

Without thinking, I said, "Mike."

"*What* did you say?" Mike asked softly.

"Who's Mike, honey?"

My other line blinked, thank God. It was Neil.

"Sorry, Mom. I gotta go."

"Ralphie—"

"Business, Mom. Don't forget to tell Uncle Al I give him my regards." I switched it over. "What's up, Neil?"

"Just got something in from that Sheffield's case. It came in about two minutes ago."

"I'm having lunch right now. Can this wait half an hour?"

"I'm just about to grab a sandwich myself. I'll prob'ly be back by one."

57

"Just give me a teensy hint of what's going on, first."

"A camera caught your Rhodes babe at the Sun Bank about ten minutes before she drove to Sheffield's."

"What was she doing?"

"She was at a drive-in ATM at her bank on Semoran, pulling money out."

"You're sure this was Sara Rhodes?"

"It sure looks like her."

"I'll be there within the hour."

"One other thing…"

"What's that?"

"She didn't look frightened."

"Are you sure it's her?"

"She was taking money out of the ATM. The camera was focused right on her face."

"The entire time?"

"Exactly."

"And she was taking money out of an ATM when someone was supposedly following her?"

"You got it."

"Interesting…"

"C'mon in. We'll talk about it."

***

After devouring my double cheeseburger and curly fries (and, as a concession to my mother, leaving the lettuce and six curly fries on the plate to reduce calorie consumption), I returned to Neil's office a few minutes after one.

Neil was sitting behind his desk when I walked in. He was finishing a French fry smothered in Ketchup. This made me wonder if his mother ever pestered him about his diet as mine did. I wanted to laugh. I couldn't imagine anyone telling Neil what not to eat.

"This is what just came in." Neil flicked on the film. It flashed on the screen of his laptop. It showed the blond goddess who'd approached me at Sheffield's. The camera was obviously positioned just above the ATM machine. She was standing in the center of the screen, looking directly at us. About fifty feet behind her, the Lexus sat at the curb. I couldn't tell for sure but wondered if I saw movement in the back seat.

Neil was right; she didn't look frightened. Worse, she had the hint of a smile on her face.

It was definitely the woman who'd approached me. The same hair, face, and outfit. "That's her, all right."

"Seen enough?"

The clock on the film said: 2:37.

"That clock's right, isn't it?"

"Accurate as hell."

"This was what? More than hours before she went to Sheffield's?"

Neil flicked the set off. "That was something else Davenport and Gaffman just found. It sheds a new light on this case and confirms what you and I were discussing earlier. The woman working the bar at Sheffield's said Rhodes came in at around three-thirty."

"She was sitting there at the bar since three-thirty?"

"Our witness said the blonde kept changing seats, too. She said the blonde was constantly being approached, so she got up and went to a different table. At around five-thirty, she finally went over to the bar. The bar was sort of empty for about twenty minutes. The evening rush hour thins out the place until around after six. She said the blonde sat there with her second or third drink. Then you walked in."

"Just two or three drinks in almost three hours?"

"That's what the woman told us."

"Did the lady remember anything about any of the others who approached Rhodes?"

"Not really. She did say there were a couple of tables of two or three guys, and when one of them went over to Rhodes, she flung him off like the plague."

"So she *was* looking for the perfect patsy."

"We were right-on about this being a setup."

"Wanna hear the topper of them all?"

"I'm sitting down, so let her rip."

"Time of death wasn't anywhere near the time you were walking away from the Lexus."

My first thought was what Mike had told me the moment she saw the body in the front seat: "*She obviously left her body long before now...*"

"Let me guess. It was at least an hour earlier?"

"Between three and five."

"Then we were absolutely right after all."

"Yep. Whoever was driving the Lexus drove it to Sheffield's at around three-thirty with the dead girl already in the car."

I laughed. "I guess we're smarter than we know, after all."

60

"Whoever did the deed put Rhodes in the Lexus, drove to an ATM, pulled out money, then drove to Sheffield's, parked, arranged the body in the back seat, then went inside to scope for a patsy."

"Why Sheffield's?"

Neil shrugged. "Doesn't matter, does it? Maybe it was a favorite bar. Maybe the parking lot was practically empty at three-thirty. Three-thirty's a good time. Between lunch and supper. Traffic's not so bad, so the killer could take his or her time in picking a place. Or maybe the place was busy and the killer figured there would be more fish in the tank. Who knows?"

"Still want me to check it out and find who did it?"

Neil picked up his coffee cup. "It's what you do, isn't it? Besides, I should think you'd want to."

"Why? Because She made me a patsy? Because she got me involved in a grisly murder? Because she got me arrested?"

"I'd say yeah to just about all the above."

"Well, the joke's on her. Shame she didn't know I'm a private eye."

"The fact that you are one, and didn't do exactly as she was counting on, really does put the joke on her. If you'd contaminated the scene and the evidence, none of this other stuff would have come out in the first place."

"That's the best way of looking at this, I guess. Still, this won't be easy. No prints and no eyewitnesses. Other than me, that is."

Neil thought that over. "The bad ones never are easy. We've got murder one, for a start. We're also

61

looking at possible kidnapping, embezzlement, grand theft auto and a slew of other felonies."

"Like I just said. Not easy."

"Deacon, you didn't get into this racket because it would be. None of us did. So dig in. Why the hell are you dragging your ass?"

"I wish I knew."

"Is it because this might involve Raguzzo's strip club? Because you might have to step on the old man's toes?"

"Why would I care about that?"

"He's your buddy, isn't he?"

"Papa Joe? He's not actually my *buddy*..."

"Don't give me that. You've gone to bat for him several times in the last five years, so don't try and convince me otherwise."

"Don't forget, he was the one responsible for putting out the hit that almost vaporized me."

"Well, he's obviously mellowed since then. Whatever happened between you two after that—"

"I did him a favor or two." I didn't like the insinuation. I knew I should expect such opinions from cops, but they just didn't know the situation. "He paid me for a job and I helped him out. Just as I'd do for any other client. That doesn't mean we've been sharing toothpaste or pillows."

Neil went silent for a few moments. Then he nodded. "Just remember that you're on your own when you venture into his domain. And also, with Davenport and Gaffman, who most likely still think you're involved. They'll be looking for any mistake you make. That means that if you get in above your head, I might not be able to help ya."

"I told you I'd tread lightly."

Neil shook his head. "Deacon, I know you. Your version of lightly is way off the charts from mine. C'mon, now. Regardless of what two detectives might or might not think of ya, you're in good standing. You gave us that stash house last year. Don't fuck up a good thing by making nice with the wrong people."

"In other words, Vega's okay, but Papa Joe's off-limits?"

"You're getting downright abusive, now…"

I sat back and sighed.

Neil finally stopped glaring. "Don't let this one get to ya."

"I just don't like being played. And I sure as hell don't like being looked at as a killer—especially when all I did was pick the wrong barstool at the wrong time."

"We've all been played once or twice…"

"That doesn't make it any better. Or easier."

"If it was that easy, any moron could do it."

"When you put it *that* way…"

"It's the only way of putting it."

I sighed. Neil was right, as usual.

"Don't forget what I said about Davenport and Gaffman, now. They're chomping at the bit to solve this one quick. In other words, they'll be looking for any excuse to nail your ass."

"I'll be as invisible as possible."

"And as quiet…"

"You're taking all the fun out of this."

"Just remember, if you find something, be careful. Don't do it yourself. Call in whatever you've got, and I'll have those two handle the collar. If they can't do the heavy lifting with this one, the entire city will hear about it."

"You're worried?"

Neil shrugged. "We're talking about a bunch that doesn't mind slitting a woman's throat. Whoever did it almost took her head clean off. This means be careful, dammit."

"Can you get me a wallet-sized copy of Sara Rhodes? I'll need it."

"No problem." He opened the folder and took out one of the copies. "I take it you're gonna start at the club…"

"I don't think I have much of a choice."

Neil nodded. "Just keep in touch, okay? I may not be able to lend a hand, but that won't stop me from trying to keep your ass outa hot water."

"That's good to know, Daddy…"

"I'm serious."

"So am I." Then I got up, left, and headed for the Trail.

Chapter 7

At a little after two o'clock that afternoon, Vesper's was enjoying the tail end of its heavy lunch crowd, which included their customary lavish seafood buffet.

The first five rows of the parking lot offered only a few empty spots, so I parked the TransAm by itself in the center of the sixth row.

"Do you have any idea what you're going to do when you go in there?" Mike had been sitting beside me since I left the Police Station. Although she was a spirit, right now she appeared more transparent than she had on the way over.

"Why are you hazier than usual?"

"Probably because I don't really like coming here. My heart—or whatever I have now in place of one—just isn't in this. It seems like every time you come here, someone beats you half to death or tries to kill you."

"Not *every* time."

"Don't forget that time that guy knocked you out, took you to their warehouse, zip-tied you to a chair and told you he was going to play a scene from one of his favorite movies, which included mashing your toes with a hammer."

"You got me out of that. Remember?"

"I had to get you out of it, didn't I? That man was crazy."

"Most of the people I have to deal with are crazy. I don't often come into contact with bookworms or Wally Cox types. The people I look for usually have something dangerous and illegal to hide and will kill rather than give up what they've been doing. I thought you knew all that."

"That's not the point. And yes, I know they're all crazy. That doesn't make me feel any better, you realize."

"Mike, nothing's gonna happen. I'm just trying to figure out what's going on."

"That doesn't answer my question."

"I forgot what it was."

"Do you know what you're going to do when you go in there?"

"To put it bluntly, no."

"I guess I figured as much."

"Go on. I know you're about to say something else."

"This doesn't give me a warm fuzzy."

"I didn't know you wanted a warm fuzzy."

"Every once in a while, it helps ease my mind."

"You're dead."

"Really?"

"You know what I mean."

"What do you mean?"

"Mike, I know you. You're much too smart not to be at least two steps ahead of me in everything I do."

"Maybe, but just so we're on the same page, explain yourself."

"You first."

"What do you mean?"

"Why would you need a warm fuzzy?"

"I need to know what you plan to do. Otherwise, I have no idea how I'll be able to help you. The way I see it, you're going inside, and while you're in there, you'll get someone angry. You'll be tossed outside or beaten up first, then tossed outside. If things look especially bad, I'm going to have to make one of those tricky nine-one-one calls—which is kind of difficult for me because I have to use much of my stored-up energy, and it drains me. If I have enough time, I'll have to just try and figure out what they're going to do to you and act accordingly. But since you seem to have the ability to get someone angry in just a second or two, I might not have enough time to plan something. Does that answer your question?"

"And then some."

"So once again...do you have any idea what you're going to do?"

"Once again, I'm going to reply no."

"None at all?"

"Other than showing the girl's picture around and asking a couple of questions, I can't do much more than that."

"I guess that'll have to do for right now."

"Her trail leads back to here."

"Well, yeah. She worked here, so..."

"She was the one found in the Lexus."

"But she wasn't the girl who approached you at Sheffield's."

"She sure looked like her. Exactly like her. Which is why I asked Neil if the dead girl had a twin."

"A twin who wore the same exact outfit?"

"I know. It's looking more and more like a complex, well-thought-out plan, doesn't it?"

"Yes. It does. And it convinces me even more that the people you're looking for are crazy. And very dangerous."

"I know they're dangerous."

"You didn't see the blood in that car."

"I can imagine."

"You've really got to be some sort of maniac to do something like that and be able to stage it so coldly."

"I'm still wondering how her killer got out of there so quickly. Short of crawling away and sneaking behind the bushes, then getting back to a getaway car, I can't think of any other way it could have been done."

"I'm sure who did it was good at sneaking away. This tells me the killer's done this type of thing before."

"I can think of something else that's equally important."

"What's that?"

"How did the tall blonde know I wouldn't try opening her door when she brought me over there in the first place? For all she knew, I could have waited until she opened the driver's door before deciding to turn around and walk away. Then I would've seen the dead girl."

"But she didn't, did she?"

"No."

"Why didn't she?"

I shrugged. "I guess she had me pegged as the type of guy who wouldn't stand there and watch."

"And if you had?"

"I'm sure she had that covered as well."

68

"I'm sure she would have told you she was okay," Mike said. "And that you could go on your way. She might have even made some comment about it that would have made you feel silly. But she didn't have to. And the moment your back was turned, she did what she needed to do."

"Cold," I said.

"And very dangerous."

"You said that before."

"And I still mean it."

***

Two human tanks wearing loose-fitting suits blocked me at the club entrance.

One of them stared at me as a Rottweiler would contemplate which part he wanted to tear off and eat first. The other held out his catcher's mitt-sized palm to take my ten-spot. Once he'd pocketed the bill, he stepped aside while his partner held the door open.

The main room displayed an odd mix of expensive suits and sweatshirts gathered in small, scattered groups in the large carpeted air-conditioned area. I slipped through staggered clots of businessmen sipping drinks and talking stocks, spreadsheets, acquisitions, and politics. I closed my ears and focused on the pulsating beat of the juke thumping wildly from the speaker system. Talk of investments, politics and all other white-collar crap always made my eyes glaze over and my brain approach major gooey meltdown. I concentrated instead on the irritating beat while scanning every available female in the room.

There were dozens of them. Vesper's boasted using the sweetest babes in the city and prided itself on the top-notch quality of its lap dancers and hostesses. Slim, sensuous, half-naked creatures balanced trays topped with drinks while others danced on the bar counter.

However, not one of them even remotely resembled the tall blonde I'd met in Sheffield's the night before.

"You actually think you'll find her here?" Mike stayed close and moved through a small cluster of guys in suits I passed.

"Not so far."

"I wouldn't think she'd work here."

"What makes you say that?"

Mike glided through a balding fat man gawking at one of the waitresses. She must have given off a spark from her aura. He flinched the moment she slipped through him. He nearly spilled his drink. "Too obvious?" she asked me.

"No doubt." I ordered a bourbon on the rocks from the bosomy brunette tending bar. After I'd paid and turned away, a tall, dark-haired, square-shouldered guy in a custom-fitting suit approached me.

"Deacon?"

I looked up at the Adam's apple nearly totally concealed amongst the corded neck muscles and noticed that he'd nicked himself shaving or playing with his stiletto. "Guilty as charged."

"Follow me."

"Why?"

70

His dark eyes blinked, but only slightly. "Because I said so."

"Is that an order?"

"More like a request."

"Even better. Where?"

Instead of replying, he just frowned and gestured for me to follow.

"What do you think?" I whispered to Mike.

"You need answers, so I think you'd better follow him."

"What if he wants to kill me?"

She smiled one of her humorless smiles. "You actually think I'll let him do that?"

"What was I thinking?"

My escort turned and gave me another frown. "Say somethin'?"

"Just thinking out loud."

"You comin' or what?"

"What if I say what?"

His one thick black eyebrow flinched. "You sayin' you ain't comin'?"

"I didn't say that."

"What *are* ya sayin'?"

"I'm just wondering what'll happen if I don't go with you?"

He stepped closer. "The boss wants to see ya."

"Well, since you asked me so nicely…" I downed my drink and placed it on the bar counter.

He turned around and led the way down the hall, where the offices were located.

***

Sitting behind his massive mahogany desk, Sonny Bergman watched me guardedly as Mike and

I went inside the exquisitely furnished, air-conditioned office.

Even seated, Sonny presented an imposing picture: yard-wide shoulders, large features, thick black hair, and large piercing black eyes.

Sonny had been running Vesper's for Papa Joe Raguzzo for nearly ten years. Papa Joe had semi-retired a couple of years earlier due to health reasons and had given Sonny free reign. The place had been doing high-volume business ever since. Although Papa Joe also owned seven other clubs in the Orlando area, three in Miami and two in Tampa, Vesper's had always been his favorite. Keeping this in mind, Sonny ran the place the best way he knew but was careful to keep things the way Papa Joe would want them. Although Papa Joe rarely came into the club nowadays, he frequently called in to talk to Sonny about how things were going.

"Sonny..." I went in and stood in front of the desk. Mike appeared right beside me, gazing at him in her disapproving way.

Sonny didn't speak right off. As always, he studied me a few moments, possibly to determine why I'd come to his place. While just about everyone else came here for the girls and the drinks, Sonny and the rest of the management knew all about me. They also understood that when I came to the club, it was most likely for business purposes. They didn't like it because they were wise guys and not great fans of cops or detectives. But they all knew my history with Papa Joe and realized that they had to put their hatred and distrust aside and treat me more or less in a civilized manner. They could still throw me out if they thought I was causing trouble, but it would have to be done "carefully," with minimal bruising and very little loss of blood.

After nearly a minute, Sonny said, "Whaddya doin' here, Deacon?"

"I'm looking for one of your girls."

"Why?"

"One of them was murdered last night at Sheffield's on Colonial Drive."

He watched me a few moments before he spoke again. "If she was murdered, why the hell would you be lookin' for 'er here?"

"You raise a good point." I didn't realize Sonny was able to figure out something like that so quickly.

He shrugged a massive shoulder. "So answer the fuckin' question."

"Such language," Mike whispered.

"I came here to find out if anyone knows what happened."

Sonny didn't reply. He looked like he was trying to burn a hole in my forehead with his steely glare.

"Did you hear about it?" I asked.

He watched me a few more moments. "Mebbe."

"I almost got murdered with her."

His expression was impassive when he said, "Shame."

"You didn't tell me you two were such close friends," Mike said flatly.

73

I tossed her a quick wink. "I knew you'd be upset," I told Sonny.

He sat back. "You'd better do somethin' about that tick."

"I know I should have a checkup, but these Florida doctors are a pain in the ass. They want you to sit in their office for three hours. I just don't have that kind of time. Besides, their chairs do a serious job on my tailbone. I've got sciatica. It flares up like a bastard when I sit too long."

"Poor baby," Mike said.

"It happens," Sonny said, looking at his nails.

"I know. Once you hit forty…" I shrugged.

"That still don't tell me why you're here."

"I thought I just did."

"Mebbe you just ain't clear enough. Try spellin' it out. No more talk about your fuckin' sciatica, okay? And talk real slow so I get it the first time."

"One of your strippers…was sitting in her car. A Lexus. Someone slit her throat…outside Sheffield's…last night." I shrugged. "How's that?"

He thought that over for a few moments. It must have taken a while for the information to travel from his ears up to his brain. "Which one?"

"Sara Rhodes."

Sonny glanced past me, where my escort was standing in front of the massive door. Sonny raised his two thick black brows. I turned to see how the other guy reacted. He just shrugged.

"We don't know who you're talkin' about, Deacon," Sonny said.

"Would a picture help?"

"You got one?"

"Now how smart would that make me look if I asked you that and didn't have one with me?"

Sonny sent over one of those expressions that suggested that he was deciding whether to answer my question or just have my escort take me outside and break one of my legs.

While he was deciding, I pulled Neil's wallet-sized shot from the inner pocket of my jacket and handed it to him.

Sonny took it carefully and studied it. He nodded and gestured with his manicured thumb for the other guy to come over. "Mebbe..." He handed it to the other guy, who glanced at it and nodded. He handed it back to his boss. "Know 'er?" Sonny asked him.

"Yeah, boss. Dusty, she went by. Seen 'er around, coupla times. One of the bar dancers."

Sonny handed the photo back to me.

"Has she been around lately?" I pocketed it.

Sonny shrugged.

The other guy shook his head. "Haven't seen 'er in two, mebbe three weeks."

"Is that normal?"

He shrugged.

"These broads, they come and go," Sonny said. "They need money, they come here, dance a few spots and split." He shrugged. "Who knows? Who the fuck cares? Besides, they all look alike to me."

"Nice guys," Mike said.

"Do they all look alike to you?" I asked my escort.

75

He nodded and went back to make sure the door hadn't budged.

"That all ya need?" Sonny asked.

"You wouldn't by any chance have an address for this girl, would you?"

Sonny's eyes narrowed. "You fuckin' with me, Deacon?"

"If she danced here, that means she was your employee." I paused a moment to let that one sink in. "Records, maybe? Time sheets? Or don't you guys bother about those pesky 1040's the rest of us have to tend to every April?"

Since Papa Joe had always been a stickler about taxes and records, I knew Sonny couldn't squirm through this one.

He opened a drawer, pulled out a rather thick black leather-bound book and opened it. He went through several pages, pressed his fat index finger to a page and slid it down a printed list, stopping about halfway down. "Says she worked here about six months, off and on, then left two weeks ago."

"How about an address?"

"All it says is Orlando."

Terrific. "That narrows it down."

Sonny shoved the book back into the drawer and slammed it shut. "That it?"

"I take it you don't care much about part-time help."

"Ya wouldn't believe how many bimbos come through this place every week."

"Let me take a wild guess. Hundreds?"

"This place has a good rep. The good ones always try us first. Can't keep track of 'em if they

76

dance for a week or so, disappear, come back a month, maybe two months later, dance another week or so, then split."

"I guess not."

Sonny shrugged. "That it?"

"I guess it'll have to do. Thanks for your time." I turned.

"Deacon?"

"Yeah?"

"Glad ya didn't get your throat cut."

"You two really *are* close friends." Mike seemed surprised.

"I am, too." I was also shocked by his statement. I watched him for a few moments to see if he was serious. I couldn't tell. Sonny rarely showed any expression but contempt, hatred, and disgust. "Really?"

"Papa Joe wouldn't like it."

I grinned. That sounded more like Sonny. "Give him my best."

Sonny nodded. Then he pulled a gold nail file from his pocket and began carefully filing one of his nails.

Chapter 8

"That was a waste of time," Mike said when we went back outside.

"It might have helped things along if Sonny wasn't such an asshole," I said.

"What's his problem? All you wanted was to find out about a dancer who worked there. His telling you about her wouldn't hurt his reputation, would it?"

"It would if he'd actually helped me…"

"I guess I don't understand."

"You don't know these guys like I do." I opened my door and we both got back into the TransAm. "They're weird about talking to cops or anyone associated with law enforcement. They've got their own code, and that usually means the same thing to all of them—don't tell anyone anything. Keep your mouth shut unless you're talking to one of your own. And unless you've got a gun pointed at your face, you stick to that code."

"But you've helped your mob friend a bunch of times."

"Papa Joe isn't my friend. Yeah, I've helped him out a time or two. But that doesn't cut any ice with these guys. They're barely operating on the side of the law, but that doesn't mean they have any respect for it. Sonny's got a sheet. So does the other guy. Everyone working at Vesper's has probably been in prison once or twice."

"So where does this leave us? You've just gone to a place where a dead stripper used to work, and they acted like they didn't even know her. All you do know is that she had an Orlando address. Where can you possibly go from here?"

"I guess it's time to use one of my contacts." I started up the ignition.

"You have contacts?" Mike sounded surprised.

"In this business, I kind of have to."

Mike looked confused. "I didn't know you had actual *contacts*."

"What do you think *you* are?"

"I'm a contact?"

"In a manner of speaking..."

"I'm dead."

"You're still a contact. My contact. My favorite contact. And most of all, my *best* contact."

She smiled. "I appreciate the flattery, but what does this have to do with finding out about that dead stripper? I'm just as in the dark about this as you are. This probably means I'm not a very good contact right now."

"Maybe not, but I know someone who might possibly shed a little light on this."

"You mean one of those unsavory people you've come across in the past?"

"Now you've got it. We've used a couple in the last few years."

Mike frowned. "I just don't like it that you even know these people."

"They come in handy."

"Which one are you going to use?"

"Well, right now I need someone who goes to Vesper's a lot. Someone who pays attention to the dancers."

79

"Then you're looking for someone who goes there a lot and who salivates over the girls?"

"I wouldn't say he actually *salivates* over them…"

"What *would* you say, then?"

"He sort of ogles them."

"He's an ogler?"

"That sounds like him."

Mike's frown remained. "I don't think I'm going to like this guy."

"Give him a chance, Mike. He just might be able to help us." I backed out of my space and eased down the gravel lane that led us back to the Trail.

***

Albert "Doodles" Mensky earned his nickname from his pencil sketches of monsters and scary animals he dreamed about years ago in college, while tripping on heroin.

He got hooked on the hard stuff shortly after graduating from high school. It eventually landed him in prison, where he'd served time for possession and intent to sell. He was released three years ago and had been working in his sister's clothing store at the Kissimmee Mall ever since. As far as I knew, he'd been off the needle for years and was working in the stockroom and keeping her store clean.

If Doodles hadn't gotten hooked on heroin, he would have probably made something of himself. He'd been just half a dozen credits short of earning two college degrees—one in Finance and the other in Economics—but went all screwy a couple of months before graduating, while cramming for finals. His addiction took over and all prospects of a promising future disappeared. Because of his weakness, no one could trust him, and despite his brilliance with math and figures, his sister didn't want him going anywhere near the cash register.

I stayed in touch with Doodles because we'd been friends for years. Since he knew what was happening on the street, he'd tell me whatever I needed to know for a few dollars. Ever since he'd gotten off the heroin, he was content doing occasional coke and daily weed. He liked the stuff moving around in the local area—particularly what he could find at Vesper's.

Everyone knew Doodles was harmless. He was a good customer and kept his mouth shut. His unkempt appearance and his aversion to daily hygiene turned people right off. Since people avoided him, he was able to score and walk away without worrying about being noticed.

Doodles lived by himself in his sister's travel trailer in her small backyard in St. Cloud. It was a perfect arrangement. He did whatever she wanted him to do and kept the trailer clean. In return, she gave him his space and even let him display some of his least offensive sketches on the walls of the trailer. He only had to work at her store four hours at a stretch— which gave him his mornings and nights free. As long as he kept his weed and coke use under control, he didn't have to answer to anyone. His restored '57 Chevy got him around. He never entertained or worried about maintaining a decent wardrobe. This kept his expenses low. He lived on pizza, Doritos, cashews and soft drinks, and knew enough about women to realize that, in his present situation, he wouldn't be considered a good catch.

Doodles figured he had the world by the short curlies. He was perfectly content, living happily in his own little world.

I parked the TransAm next to his restored '57 Chevy at the far end of the big brick building. There were a few noticeable rusty spots on the rear quarter panel I hadn't noticed the last time I'd talked with him. I figured he was low on cash or no longer cared about keeping his classic ride in mint condition. Knowing him as I did, I decided he was probably spending too much money on coke and weed. This might suit me just fine. He could probably use some extra cash. It didn't take much to get Doodles talking.

"What's this contact's name?" Mike asked as we got out of the TransAm.

"Doodles."

She grimaced. "I hope that's just a nickname..."

"His real name's Albert, but he hates it."

"He hates Albert? But likes Doodles?"

I nodded.

"Albert's a nice name."

"You think so?"

"It seemed to work for Einstein and Schweitzer."

"It didn't work so well with Albert Fish..."

"Who?"

"The real-life Hannibal Lecter."

"You can be *so* obnoxious..."

82

"You're beginning to sound like my mother again."

"I'm beginning to understand her more and more by the day."

A thick cloud of gray dust flew up behind one of the dumpsters. Doodles appeared, pushing a long-handled broom lazily along the loading dock floor. He was singing to himself as usual. I couldn't hear what the tune was, but his favorite had always been "Stairway to Heaven." Every once in a while, he stopped what he was doing and reached up to push a clump of shoulder-length mousey-brown hair over his shoulder.

Doodles had never been one to multi-task, preferring to do things one at a time. He wore a black tee shirt with something painted in white on the front, as well as on the back. From our angle, I couldn't make out what it was. He also wore faded jeans with the knees ripped out and battered black tennis shoes that looked like they'd been buried in soft mud and put back on without being hosed off. He'd missed some dirt on his way over to the end of the dock. Noticing it, he stopped moving and just stared at it. He seemed to be debating what he should do, then shrugged and walked away from it.

"You sure you want to ask him questions?" Mike asked.

"Why?"

"No offense, but I don't know if he could handle communication from an actual human being right now."

"I think he'll be all right."

"He looks, well, strange."

83

"He's definitely strange. But that's only because he's usually high on something when he's awake."

"Which is he now? Awake? Or asleep?"

"Are you trying to be silly?"

"Actually, I think *you're* the silly one if you intend to question him right now."

"Give him some credit, okay?"

"I'm trying to, believe me."

"You could've fooled me."

"Right now, I think I'm fooling myself because I can't really tell what's going on with him."

"Like I said, give him a little credit. He's shown signs of remarkable intelligence at times."

Doodles abruptly stopped walking. He bent over, picked up something from the ground, sniffed it, put it close to his ear and listened. Then said something to it. A moment later he dropped it, straightened, stepped on it and resumed walking.

Mike frowned. "This isn't one of those times, is it?"

I had to admit that the boy wasn't making a good case for himself. "Obviously not."

Mike nodded. "I thought maybe I was imagining things."

"Give the guy a break, okay? Who knows? We might learn something here."

Just then, Doodles turned and saw me. He began squinting. It made me wonder if his eyesight was going or if the sun was in his eyes. He looked like he hadn't been awake very long. "Deakhead? That you?"

84

"*Deak*head?" Mike was giving me one of her looks.

"That's a nickname, too," I whispered. "Dood!" I waved.

"Dood and Deakhead..." Mike shook her head. "This is going to be interesting."

He leaned on the broom handle as I approached him. "Slummin' again?"

"Something like that. I need to talk to you about something."

"Somethin' important?"

"Very."

"Somethin' worth actual *money*?"

"I'd say so."

"*Real* money?"

"I never carry Monopoly money with me anymore. Most people usually clam up and look at me funny when I take it out of my pocket."

He pushed more hair over his shoulder. Since our view was no longer obscured, the sketch on his tee shirt was quite clear. It was an airbrush study of a giant cockroach devouring a handful of scurrying rats. The artwork was good, the subject matter disgusting. I could tell Mike wasn't impressed; she'd turned away.

"How much?"

"Twenty."

Doodles shook his head. "Not much bread, man."

"This shouldn't take more than five minutes of your time. Five minutes for twenty bucks? That's two hundred and forty bucks an hour. What's your sister paying you?"

85

"Ten bucks an hour…"

"Not bad, right?"

"Man…" He made a sour face.

I could tell by his expression that he wasn't buying it. It wasn't very bright of me to do math estimates with a guy possessing his qualifications.

"I'm on a case, and I think it might involve Vesper's."

He squinted. "Vesper's?"

"That big, fancy yellow and pink building that looks like a casino. You go there all the time. It's covered with bright lights and has booze, huge bouncers, and beautiful half-naked girls inside. It's also got some people there who'll sell you anything. You know what I'm talking about, don'tcha, Dood? Weed? Coke? Shit like that?"

His thick brown brows bumped together. "Gotcha. *That* Vesper's…"

"Great. Now that we're on the same page, I need you to tell me a few things about—"

"Sure it's just for twenty?"

"What's wrong with twenty?"

"Not much. As long as I don't get fucked up."

"Whaddya mean?"

"The dudes there are bad, man. They're really big. And nasty. Real nasty. I get fucked up, I can't do my work here, and Carol'll be pissed—and I mean *fucking* pissed."

"How's thirty sound?"

"Better'n twenty."

"Good."

Doodles grinned. "I'll bet ya think I forgot all about what I learned in college, huh?"

86

Mike gave me one of her half-smiles. "I guess this is one of those examples of remarkable intelligence you told me about…"

I ignored her. "Not for a second," I told Doodles.

"Thirty, then. But if anything I say gets me fucked up or tossed out, you're gonna have to deal with Carol, and she can get really ugly." His eyes grew. "I mean ugly, man."

"I get it."

"I mean butt-ugly. Pit-bull ugly. Twisted insides ugly—"

"I think I understand, Dood."

Doodles was on a roll. "I don't need to be fucked up, man. I like my head to get fucked up. Not the rest of me."

I pulled out my wad and peeled off three tens. "I need to find out about someone who used to work there."

He studied the three tens. "Lots of people work there, man."

"This one was a dancer."

He tilted his head as if he had no idea what I'd just said.

"One of those skinny ladies who comes out on stage in a skimpy two-piece, does a few sexy moves, then takes it all off and then—"

"I know about strippers, man."

"Good. The one I'm looking for is dead."

He swallowed. "*Dead*-dead?"

"Deader than a cooter."

"*That* dead?"

"Throat was cut."

87

He blinked. "Ya mean—"

I simulated the throat-cut gesture with my index finger.

His eyes grew. "A regular knife thingy?"

"He's quick," Mike said.

"You got it."

"Know who did it?"

"Not yet. I have to find out what she was into. Then maybe it'll all come out."

He opened his palm. "Twenty more, man. This is heavy-duty shit. This kinda shit'll get me dusted."

I gave him another twenty. "I don't think you'll get into any trouble just by telling me about her…"

"Ya sure about that?"

"Reasonably." I took Neil's photo out of my pocket and handed it to him.

He squinted at it for a moment. Then he nodded. "That's Dusty." He took a breath. "*Dusty's* the one…who bought it?"

"You've seen her before?"

"Nice babe. Skinny, but her jugs were really nice. Skinny babes always have lousy pancake jugs. Not Dusty, no siree. When she was dancin' on the bar, she'd balance a quarter on one of 'em, then arch her back and send it flyin' up, and she could catch it in her mouth."

"That sounds great, Dood."

"She was really classy," Mike said flatly.

I pocketed the photo. "Have you seen her with anyone backstage?"

"Backstage?"

"Where you usually have to go to score."

Doodles looked sheepish. "You mean a guy thingy?"

"I'm looking for anyone—a guy or a babe—who you might have seen with this girl."

He contemplated the money in his fist. "Kinda light, dude…"

"Make believe it's bigger."

He giggled. "Maybe if I imagined hair around it…"

"Whatever turns your crank…"

Mike sighed. "This is *so* high school. And *so* stupid…"

After a moment, Doodles said, "I did see a dude with her two or three times. He was with her the last time I saw her. It was outside in the parkin' lot, maybe a week or so ago. Mighta been two weeks, actually."

"The same guy?"

A nod. "I never saw him inside the place. He gave ya the impression he didn't wanna be seen."

"What makes you say that?"

"He sorta kept his back to the parkin' lot and didn't look at the bouncer dudes directly. He wore shades and a baseball cap. Which was weird."

"Why weird?"

"Shades? At night?"

"Ah. I get it. Go on."

"Anyway, this dude looked nervous. Or pissed."

"Can you describe him?"

A shrug. "Really tall. Red hair. About forty."

I waited, but he didn't elaborate. That wasn't much of a description. "That's it?"

"It was dark, but I did get a look at him when he was gettin' into his car."

"What kind of car?"

He shrugged. "New. Pricey. I can't tell models anymore."

"Did you catch the color?"

"Dark."

"Was it by any chance a muscle car?"

He shook his head. "He wasn't the muscle car kind. He was more of a snooty kinda dude that likes showin' off."

This was getting a *little* better, but I still couldn't go very far with it.

"Want a sketch?"

"Can you do one?"

"I'm good, Deak." He pointed to his shirt. "See?"

"I know, Dood. I just didn't know if you still did that sort of stuff."

A shrug. "It keeps the nightmares away."

"Really?"

"I get a nightmare. When I draw what was in it, I don't have it anymore."

I pointed to his shirt. "You actually dreamed that?"

He grinned. "But not anymore."

"That's the weirdest kind of therapy I've ever heard," Mike said with a sigh.

Dood reached into his back pocket and pulled out a small notepad and pencil. He opened the pad and started scribbling. Less than a minute later, he ripped off the sheet and handed it to me.

I frowned. So did Mike.

90

It was the cartoon character of a stick figure with a huge, round head and the face of someone resembling a young Anthony Hopkins. He was wearing a suit and tie.

"What the hell is this?"

"That's him." Doodles pocketed his pad and pencil.

"Dood, this is a cartoon character."

A shrug. "That's what the dude looks like."

"Ask him if he was high when he saw the man," Mike said.

"Were you high when you saw this guy?"

"Always, man. I gotta be when I go inside to score. Otherwise, I'll do somethin' stupid, and they'll toss me out."

I just stared at him. I was frustrated with the caricature but figured Doodles was trying to help in his own unique way. It wouldn't be very nice to take my money back and yell at him, so I just nodded. "Anything else you can tell me?"

"Not really, man. Like I said, that's the dude. I mean, he stood out—even though he wouldn't go inside and stayed away from the spots out in front." He shrugged. "He shows up in a nice suit but doesn't wanna go on inside. Then Dusty comes out for one of her breaks and they talk for a little. Then they start arguin', and she runs right back inside."

"And what did he do then?"

Doodles shrugged. "He stood there a little while. Then he pulled out his phone and tried makin' a call."

"Tried?"

"Whoever he called didn't answer. Pissed him off, so he stuck the phone back in his pocket and went back to his car."

"That's all you saw?"

"That was it. I saw him at least twice, maybe three times, but he never noticed me. No one does. That's cool, 'cause I'm usually there just long enough to score. I like lookin' at the babes, too, but that's no biggie. I'm one of those dudes no one sees, but I know a sweet babe when I see one. Like I said, I don't bother anyone when I'm there. I just buy a nickel bag, step outside and smoke a blunt, then go back inside and try to score some coke—*Whoa!*" He let go of the broom and stepped back abruptly. The broom handle dropped sharply onto the concrete.

"What's wrong?"

Doodles was staring directly at Mike. His jaw had dropped. He rubbed his eyes, shook his head and pulled his hair away from his face.

"Dood?"

"Wow, man…" He was squinting. "For a sec, I thought I saw somethin' there!"

I glanced nervously at Mike. "What did you see?"

"Well, it looked just like…a *babe*!"

"A babe?"

"Yeah. *Wow*… Nice, too. Hotter than a firecracker! Standin' right there, beside you!"

"Still see her?"

He squinted. "Naw, just a flash, and then *poof*…" He rubbed his eyes again. "Musta been that last line I had. Did it in the shitter 'bout half an hour before I came out here to sweep up. Fucks me up, ya know?"

"I can imagine…"

He shook his head. "Damn shame… Babe was so totally hot. I mean smokin'!"

"Maybe it was because we were talking about the Dusty lady."

He shrugged but didn't look convinced.

Carol came out into the loading dock. She was heavier than I remembered and looked really angry in her smart brown plaid business suit. She glared at me and immediately focused on Doodles. "You told me you'd be out here fifteen minutes, Albert. Get your ass in there now. UPS truck'll be here shortly. There's a fresh shipment of shoes I need you to unload. Now quit assin' around with this guy and get the hell in there!" She gave me another glare. Then spun around and stomped back inside.

Doodles shook his head and bent to pick up his broom.

"I guess you've just been summoned," I said.

He straightened and puffed. "I *hate* it when she calls me Albert."

"She never calls you Doodles?"

"Thinks it's stupid."

"Fancy that," Mike said.

Doodles started to turn then stopped. He blinked. "You just say somethin', Deak?"

I swallowed. "Don't tell me you're hearing voices, now…"

"Damn coke, it really fucks me up—ya know?"

"Apparently…"

93

Then, dragging the broom behind him, he shuffled back toward the rear of the store.

Chapter 9

As I took the TransAm down the main drag, I noticed Mike staring at me and giving me that look that all men dread.

This was the expression women used when they wanted the guy to realize that he was not only an idiot, but also that he'd totally disgusted her by doing or saying the world's stupidest thing. It didn't matter that Mike was dead. She was still a female. But even so, she still knew how and when to use "the look." She also knew how to pull it off.

As a result, I felt stupid and didn't even know why.

But instead of giving her the satisfaction of knowing that I was aware of what was going on, I decided to let her bring it up. I was pretty sure this had something to do with my talk with Doodles. Doodles, after all, was an acquired taste. Even so, I thought she was slightly off-base with her evaluation of him. Doodles might indeed be a wreck, but he was a talented wreck, and I was pretty sure his sketch was an accurate picture of the man he'd seen arguing with Dusty Rhodes. His drawing was probably way unrealistic, but I didn't want to totally dismiss it. In this business, a top-notch private eye couldn't afford to dismiss anything.

Especially when there was nothing else to go on.

I managed to drive all the way back to the Trail without letting Mike dive right in with her evaluation. But after two additional miles of silence, I began getting uncomfortable.

Reluctantly I decided to break the silence. I told myself that this didn't make me the weaker person. I just didn't want to spend the rest of the drive talking to myself.

Besides, I needed her input.

"I hope you're going to start talking to me again," I said.

"Why?"

"I don't like it when we don't talk."

"Sometimes silence is better."

"What are you saying?"

"I just said—"

"I heard what you said."

"Then what would you prefer I say?"

"Saying what's on your mind would be a good start."

"You really want to know what I'm thinking?"

"I know that whatever it is, it probably involves Doodles."

She didn't reply.

"I'm right. Admit it."

"Do you really want to know what I think of your contact?"

I didn't like the way she'd said the word "contact." She'd said it the same way she might have said "mental condition."

"I think I already do. And did you have to say it like that?"

"Like what?"

"You know what I mean."

She sighed. "In this case—"

96

"Come on, Mike. Give the poor guy a break. You let me know your opinion when you first saw him. And then you made comments about the way he acted. I could tell he didn't exactly impress you."

"Do you think that maybe I began feeling this way when he started talking to the stuff he was sweeping up?"

I knew better than reply to that.

"Or do you think I might have started having doubts when he made his cartoon sketch?"

"Since you brought it up—"

"He was hallucinating when he was at Vesper's. We both know that."

"Why do you say that? Because he made a caricature of a suspect?"

"*That's* what you think that was?"

"It was a good one, too."

"Seriously? A skinny, seven-foot-tall Anthony Hopkins? In a *suit*?"

"What's wrong with a suit? Even crazies dress up once in a while. Look at Sonny Bergman. And that ape guarding the door. You can't judge a guy just because he wears a suit."

"The suit is not what's bothering me."

"What is, then?"

"You're really serious about what I think?"

"Of course I am."

"It didn't look like a real person. It looked like someone hallucinating over Anthony Hopkins."

"That's how he saw this guy."

"For all you know, he might have just seen one of those Hannibal Lecter movies you like so much. Or dreamed about one."

97

"In other words, you want me to rip it up just because—"

"I never said you should rip it up…"

"Then what are we talking about?"

"I think the best thing would be to try and use it to figure out who it is. If there *is* such a person…"

"Really?"

She nodded.

"So then you think Doodles might not be as messed up as—"

"Oh, he's messed up, all right. We both know that. He's probably even psychotic. I just think we shouldn't shoot this down just because it's a cartoon sketch. I could be wrong, but I have to assume that he might have actually seen this man and drawn him the way he saw him at the time."

"That's what I was thinking." Something suddenly occurred to me. "Tell me something."

"All right…"

"How the hell did he see *you*?"

"I have no idea."

"He saw you, ya know…"

"I know."

"Think it was all that shit he smokes and snorts that has been melting down his brain cells?"

"It would have to be. If he hallucinates, then yes, he might have been able to actually get a glimpse of me."

"You didn't purposely let him see you, did you?"

"Why would I?"

"I don't know. Maybe you relaxed for a second, and he picked up on a vibe or two that made it possible for him to get a slight glimpse of you."

"I didn't relax at all. It didn't even occur to me. If I had, who knows what he would have done?"

"You're right. But he saw you. And as you really are."

"What do you mean?"

"He saw you as I see you."

"How's that?"

"He said you were hotter than a firecracker."

"Stop."

"Doesn't that tell you anything?"

"What should it tell me?"

"If he saw you as you are and as I see you, what makes you think he didn't see the guy with Dusty?"

"We don't know his mental condition when he saw this man."

"He did say he always went into Vesper's sober."

"You believe him?"

"I know Doodles. He doesn't drive when he's high. He thinks too much of his ride to risk driving in that condition."

"He also said he was outside when he saw him."

"So?"

"Maybe he'd done something once he scored inside the club."

"He still had to drive home…"

"Maybe he just had a little. Or maybe he had a little more than that and decided to sleep it off in his car."

"That's possible, I guess…"

"He could have bought his supply, went outside and saw that man while he was getting high."

"You could be right."

"So why are you arguing with me so much?"

"I'm just trying to keep a perspective on this."

"We've got other things to worry about."

"You're right. I just paid fifty bucks for a cartoon version of Anthony Hopkins."

"A tall, young, skinny Anthony Hopkins."

"I guess things could be worse." I had to force myself to think that Doodles hadn't been totally nutso when he'd worked up the sketch.

"So what's next?"

"I can do one of two things. First of all, I can take this sketch to Neil and see if he can figure something out by putting it into the system. Or I can do something that could turn out to be kind of dangerous."

"Another trip to Vesper's?"

"What do *you* suggest?"

"I suggest you do what your instinct tells you to do."

"You're my instinct."

"I didn't realize you thought so much of me."

"I do. I always did. I always will. So…?"

"Since that first option won't land you in the hospital and could quite possibly help find us a clue, I suggest we drive to the Police Department first to see if your rude police buddy can glean something out of that sketch."

"And if that doesn't work?"

"Then we'll have to try that strip club again and see if we can get you out of there in one piece."

"Mike, you're a lady after my own heart."

"Let's just hope those nasty wise guys don't get the chance to rip it out first."

***

"Why the hell am I looking at a cartoon sketch of that Hannibal Lecter guy?" Neil glared at Doodles' drawing. "Is this a joke?"

In this case, I was glad Mike had chosen not to come in with me. Good thing she didn't like Neil. Otherwise, I'd be forced to stand there while she laughed at me.

"It's a sketch of a guy who might be connected with Sara Rhodes."

Neil pulled it closer to his face. He shook his head and dropped it on the blotter. "Who the hell did this?"

"A contact of mine."

Neil thought that one over. "This contact... He living on his own? Or did ya have to check in to one of the local sanitariums to see him?"

"I admit that he gets high."

"This looks like a hallucination—or a drug high."

I sat down in the chair facing his desk. "Maybe, but he's extremely talented. He's really quite an artist. He can draw just about anything."

"Then why didn't he draw something that looks like an actual human being?"

"Neil, there must be something you can get out of that sketch..."

Neil sat back and frowned at it again.

"You can't put that in the system and see what comes out?"

"You're serious?"

"We really don't have much else to go on."

"Well, since Davenport and Gaffman haven't come up with anything lately…"

"It's worth a try, isn't it?"

Neil picked up his coffee cup. "Actually, we've done something like this before."

"Something like what?"

"Found a suspect from a cartoon sketch…"

"You're saying your artists have worked with caricatures in the past?"

He nodded.

"Then what's different about this?"

"Correct me if I'm wrong, but it's a tad extreme."

"I admit that, but if you can just get them to concentrate on the face…"

Neil studied the sketch. "Hell, it might work..."

"What might work?"

"Our artists work with Photoshop. Yeah, I guess they might be able to work up something outa this. A couple of our guys still work with sketches because, like a lot of us oldsters, they're not totally convinced with technology or computers. No guarantees, but lemme see if they can do something with this. Good enough?"

"Good enough."

Chapter 10

While waiting to hear from Neil, I headed east on Colonial and stopped at one of the many burger places on the stretch.

I ordered a bacon cheeseburger, seasoned fries, and iced tea at the takeout window. Then I paid, drove over to a vacant space toward the front of the lot, switched off the ignition and opened my bags to have my dinner.

While I ate, I watched the gleaming maroon Corvette convertible parked in a space straight across from me and tried to imagine if the owner was male or female. If it was a female, I wondered what she looked like.

"Where are you?" Mike asked as I bit into my burger. "Thinking about your friend's sketch?"

"What makes you think I'm thinking about anything?"

"Your expression."

"What about it?"

"It says you're thinking about something."

"You know me too well."

"So what are you thinking about?"

"I'm wondering if that beautiful maroon number over there belongs to a stacked blonde."

"You're sick."

"Just a healthy guy with raging hormones."

"Same thing."

"You think all healthy guys with raging hormones are sick?"

"In this case? Yes."

"Why?"

"Don't you think that since the last stacked blonde you came across nearly got you killed, you should hold off on women you don't know? At least for a little while?

"You've definitely got a valid point."

"I think you should focus on more important things and stop acting like a horny juvenile."

"I'm definitely not a juvenile."

"You don't want me to finish that thought, do you?"

"Is this your way of telling me I should keep my mind on this case?"

"I was only trying to be subtle."

"I appreciate the thought." I had a swig of tea.

"It's hard being subtle with you. I'm not exactly your mother, you know."

"My mother's still alive."

"That's not what I meant."

"I know what you meant."

"What did I mean?"

"You'd love to be blunt with me once in a while, wouldn't you?"

"Sometimes you need it tossed at you."

"Sometimes I can figure things out on my own."

"Sometimes you do things like that very well."

"Thank you."

A tall, skinny guy around thirty years old, wearing shorts and an oversized mauve sweatshirt, carried a white bag over to the beautiful maroon number and got in. He sported a blond brush cut and had some chin hair that looked bleached. My heart sank.

"Are you going over there right now and ask him out?" Mike asked. "Or are you going to just jot down his license plate number and look him up later on, when you're free and have more time?"

"Funny, Mike."

"I thought it was kind of amusing."

"I'll bet."

"Only because you deserved it..."

I finished my burger. Meanwhile, a short, skinny, small-breasted female about thirty-five years old got out of a small lime-green compact about five spaces down. Her flaming red hair, tied in a thick ponytail, flounced on her back as she hurried into the eatery.

"Are you going to salivate over her, too?" Mike asked.

"Actually, I'm kind of finished salivating for today."

"The blond guy did you in, I suppose..."

I sighed. "You need to work on your gloating."

"I didn't think my gloating needed work."

"If you just could reel some of it in occasionally... Just to spare this guy's feelings a tad."

Mike smiled. "I'll keep that in mind."

"Thank you."

My cell buzzed. It was Neil.

"What's up?"

"We might have something on your cartoon character."

"Terrific. And you were fairly fast with it, too."

"What the hell do ya mean? We've got other work going on here, too, ya know."

"No offense."

"Just get here when ya can. I'm here till six."

"Give me twenty minutes. Traffic's pretty bad right now."

***

The police photo Neil handed me looked good.

The man in the photo didn't look quite like Anthony Hopkins, but he somehow strongly resembled the caricature Doodles had sketched for me.

Mike decided to keep her opinions of Neil in check and agreed to come in with me. I was glad she did. She even agreed with the result of the search. As she stood beside me, her beautiful, hazy face just inches away, she shook her head. "Fancy that. Your spaced-out friend actually got him down."

"Told you," I said.

"I'm sorry for doubting you," she replied.

"Howzat?" Neil asked.

"Just thinking out loud."

Neil frowned. "Don't give me that. You were looking at your right arm."

I shrugged. "Old football injury."

"You played football?"

"Most guys play football in high school. Junior high. Whaddya expect?"

Neil continued frowning. "Why were you talking to it?"

"Sometimes the pain settles down when I say something to it."

"How come you never mentioned it before?"

"I never wanted to burden you with snippets from my tragic past."

Neil groaned. "Even when you provide good evidence, you have to turn into a total shithead and make with the bad jokes."

"It's always been my nature to provide bad jokes with good evidence. People tend to remember things easier. But as far as being a shithead?" I smiled sheepishly. "Everyone's got their problems."

Neil turned back to the photo. "Anyway, we've got a guy working for us who's obsessed with graphic novels. He's young—still on the right side of forty—and always has a stack of 'em on his desk. Reads 'em whenever he's on break or during slow periods. He also likes doing caricatures of real people and has quite a collection from his college days. He took your friend's work and just entered it in the system, narrowing it down with variables and doing some cross-referencing. He sat there for an hour, until he got a hit. This is what he got."

"Who *is* this guy?"

"Name's Reid Johnston. He's forty-two and calls himself a land developer, but he's had a few scrapes with the law in the last ten years. Petty stuff—assault, a coupla DUI's, and he was also brought in last year for driving without a license. There's also an embezzlement case he rolled on three, maybe four years ago. Charges didn't stick and were later dropped. Like I said, petty stuff."

"Any idea what he was doing with Dusty?"

Neil raised both sandy brows. "Whaddya think?"

107

"You mean the usual stuff?"

"Guy with money hitting on a stripper? Old school, Deacon."

"In this case, we're talking about a stripper who was murdered in an expensive, top-of-the-line car and then taken to a busy bar so she could be found with the right random patsy."

"We still have Davenport and Gaffman working on it, but they're not able to put together enough evidence to solve this one. At least, not yet. I'm getting pretty close to pulling 'em off. I was hoping you'd find more evidence before I pull the plug."

"Give me twenty-four hours and I might come up with something."

"Sure you can?"

"No promises, but I'll try."

Neil rubbed his eyes. "Since you're the one brought in the sketch, I'll give ya that."

"You didn't show this to Davenport and Gaffman?"

He shrugged. "I wasn't in the mood to put up with Davenport's bullshit. Anyway, I thought I'd give ya first crack at it."

"Then I guess Johnston will be my next stop. I think we've got to start with this guy's reason for being at Vesper's in the first place."

"I'd say right off that he didn't go there because he was bored..."

"I'm trying to ignore the obvious, Neil. Work with me here."

"I thought I was. The Vesper's thing sounds pretty obvious to me."

108

"I'm just trying to find a different explanation without sounding like a horny pervert."

"What kind of pervert do ya wanna sound like, Deacon?"

"The kind that'll eventually solve this case, of course..."

"It doesn't take a brain surgeon to figure out why guys go for strippers."

"No, but not every guy going after a stripper is seen with her just days before she's found in her car with her throat cut from ear to ear."

"Good point."

"Tell me more about him."

"Johnston owns and runs an investment office on South Semoran Boulevard. It's called L&J Investment Group, Inc. It's a small office in a strip mall just south of Gatlin. Look into it and find out what the hell's going on."

"What about Davenport and Gaffman? Still keeping them in the dark? At least for now?"

"I'm giving you the heads-up first. I kinda think this needs a lower profile than sending two detectives over there and upsetting the works."

"Anything else I should know?"

"It's a relatively new business, just two years old. Johnston also has interests in Foreman Construction, another relatively new company that isn't far from his investment offices. It's also got a South Semoran address. Other than that, there's nothing about it that raises flags."

"I guess I'll check it out and see what's going on."

"Tread lightly. For all we know, Johnston could be running a legitimate business."

"You honestly think that?"

"No, but unless you turn something up that suggests anything else, I more or less have to…"

"You know I'm bound to find out something that won't hold water."

"That's what you do, Deacon. You sniff around and stick your nose into things that are bound to get you hurt or worse. That's your business. You do it very well, actually."

"Thanks."

"Just don't do anything that'll get you hauled over to Michigan Avenue in a body bag."

"I'll make sure that doesn't happen," Mike said.

I gave her another quick wink. "I didn't think you cared."

"I don't. I just don't like paperwork."

"Neil, I've told you this before. You're nothing but a big sack of warm mush."

"Can it, Deacon. And for God's sake, get that nervous twitch checked out."

Chapter 11

Before driving to L&J Investments that night, I went back to my South Conway condo, showered, changed clothes, and checked my .380 Beretta Cheetah.

I hoped I wouldn't have to use the gun in the first place but figured I'd take it with me. I knew I probably wouldn't be able to get into the building with it, but it made me feel a little better, knowing I'd have it with me if I needed to protect myself. I usually stayed away from cases involving vicious killers, but since I'd been dragged into this one, I didn't have much choice but to solve it. Besides, Neil was counting on me. I couldn't let him down.

"You probably won't need that," Mike said, appearing on the bed beside me.

"I like to have it with me just in case."

"You have me instead. Isn't that enough?"

"When you're dealing with scum, you never know what's going to come up."

"I understand. I just think you should trust me."

"I do. More than you can imagine."

"But you're taking the gun anyway?"

"Yep."

"To feel more secure?"

"And to shoot back if someone starts shooting at me."

"I think I understand."

"I hope so."

"I still don't know why you think you'll need it with me around."

111

"What can you do if someone takes out a gun and shoots me?"

"You think I'll just stand there and let you get shot?"

"Even you have limitations, Mike."

"Name one."

"You're dead."

"How is that a limitation?"

"Well, you can't exactly take the gun away from him, can you? Or trip him before he gets one off?"

"Maybe not, but I've done other things that have gotten you out of a lot of trouble. I've saved your life many times. Did you forget any of that?"

I couldn't possibly forget any of the things Mike had done for me. Still, I couldn't help thinking that I'd be venturing into troublesome waters. I'd possibly be getting close to someone who has no qualms about slitting people's throats. This alone was enough to convince me that I should bring along my own firepower.

"Well?" Mike was waiting. "You're taking entirely too long to answer a simple question."

"I'll never forget any of the amazing stuff you've done."

"What's the problem, then?"

"Just in case you need a recharge and something bad happens while you're gone."

"I'm never very far away, you know."

I stared at the Beretta. "I know, but I still think I'd better take it. Just in case."

"If it makes you feel better. But I promise you won't need it."

I clipped the holster to my belt and shoved the Beretta into it. "Hate me for that?"

Mike smiled. "Not *too* much..."

***

We reached the front paved lot of L&J Investments on South Semoran Boulevard by seven o'clock.

At that time, the small parking lot was nearly empty. Just four vehicles were parked out front, near the glass door. Two of them were BMW's, the third a compact, and the fourth an older model black Camaro.

"Something about that Camaro is giving me bad vibes," Mike said.

"You're sure about that?"

"I'm nothing but spirit now, Ralph. Vibes are a big thing with me. Especially bad ones."

I parked the TransAm about six spaces down, next to a Chinese takeout place that had already closed. L&J looked like it had closed for the workday. Since I was already here, I had to check it out.

A large, square-shouldered uniformed guard in his mid-fifties appeared from behind some potted plants in front of the L&J entrance. I couldn't tell if he'd been hiding or just standing in front of the door next to the block wall, where we couldn't see him. He watched me closely as I flicked off the ignition.

"Maybe it *was* smart of you to bring your gun," Mike said.

"Actually, he might not be interested in me at all. We probably just woke him up from his nap."

"That's harsh."

113

"Tell me why a developer would need an armed guard."

"They all use them now, don't they? People are crazy nowadays. They'll steal anything."

"What can an investment company have that's worth stealing? I don't think they'd keep actual money in their offices."

"I think you'd need to be a thief to know something like that."

"What bothers me is that this guy looks like he doesn't mind using his piece."

"How can you tell?"

"He just lifted the hammer loop on his holster."

"So?"

"He did it without looking."

"And that means…?"

"One, he's done it hundreds of times before, so it's natural to him."

"And two?"

"He likes doing it."

"Just don't let him think you're armed, right?"

"I'll try real hard."

"I know you. You'd better try even harder."

"Thanks loads."

"I'm just looking out for you, you know."

"Sometimes you make me feel helpless, Mike."

"Are you saying you want me to disappear?"

"You'll never hear me say anything like that."

"Then just what are we talking about?"

"I'm speaking nonsense. You, on the other hand, are trying to make sense out of it."

"You're just nervous."

"A little. I like guns, but not when I might be staring down the wrong end of one."

"You'll be fine. Just don't do anything stupid."

"Define stupid."

"Anything that could get you beaten up or cause him to grab his gun."

"You've obviously forgotten what I do for a living."

"I'm just trying to stay optimistic."

"I'm glad one of us is." Then, as I opened the door to get out, the guard walked over and stood about ten feet away, his right hand on the butt of his holstered piece.

***

"State your business."

The meaty part of the guard's right hand fidgeted as it rested on the Pachmayr grip of his piece. Since the gun was hidden by the leather holster, I couldn't tell what kind it was. I could tell it was an automatic, but other than its size—which looked slightly large for the holster—I couldn't distinguish its make or caliber. The important thing was that I knew that whatever caliber it was, it would easily kill me. I was glad I was wearing my lightweight jacket. It concealed the Beretta. In this situation, it was a good thing. The guard might not pull his piece if he didn't consider me a threat. If he did, I was toast. I wouldn't be able to bring my gun out in time—not when the guard already had his hand on his own piece.

I knew to be very careful.

"I came to see Mr. Johnston."

"He ain't in."

115

I glanced at the BMW and tried a gamble. "Isn't that his car?"

The guard didn't respond right off. I'd obviously flustered him with my question. But his reaction did tell me what I needed to know. After about ten seconds, he scowled. "Just 'cause his car's here don't mean he can see ya. Who are ya, by the way?"

"My name's Deacon. I'd like to ask him a few questions about something that happened last night."

He blinked.

"Do you remember if he was here last night?"

"He's always here till seven, eight o'clock— sometimes later."

"Was last night one of his later nights?"

He continued scowling. I figured I was putting a little too much pressure on his brain cells. After a long pause, he said, "You'll have to ask *him* about that."

"But you won't let me see him."

"That means you'll have to come back, don't it?"

"I guess so."

He didn't reply. He was obviously waiting for me to leave. His hand hadn't budged from his pistol.

"I believe he might know what happened."

"Whazzat?"

"I just told you something happened last night. This is why I need to talk to him. Did you forget already?"

"Like I said, he ain't available."

"Actually, you said he ain't in."

116

"Same thing."

"Not really."

He stiffened. I was really getting to him. "Huh?"

"First you said, "He ain't in." Then you said, "Just 'cause his car's here don't mean he can see ya." Then you told me I'll have to come back. After that, you said—"

"I know what I said, Mac. He ain't—"

"Deacon."

"Howzat?"

"The name's Deacon. Not Mac."

"Whatever. Like I said, he ain't gonna talk to ya, so you can take that smartass attitude outa here right now, or—"

"If you're asking me to leave, I can take a hint."

His scowl didn't ease up at all. "Like I said already, Mr. Johnston can't see anyone right now. He's about to close up for the day."

I wanted to ask him why he didn't say that in the beginning, but as soon as I opened my mouth, I heard Mike's voice.

"He's watching you from his office." Mike drifted toward me from the direction of the building. "The Johnston guy. He looks nervous."

"I'll bet."

"Whazzat?" The guard was scowling again.

I glanced at my watch. "It's getting kind of late. Shame I couldn't have come earlier. But then we wouldn't have had such a meaningful discussion, eh?"

117

The guard just watched me as I turned back to the TransAm and got behind the wheel. Before I closed the door, I turned back to him. "Give Mr. Johnston my regards. And tell him I'll probably be back to see him tomorrow, sometime before lunch. Tell him to dress smartly. First impressions, right?" I flicked on the ignition, backed up and eased back out onto Semoran Boulevard.

Just as I joined the heavy northern flow, I turned to Mike. "You're sure that was Johnston?"

"He looked just like your friend's sketch."

"Great. Was there anything else you found out?"

"He was on the phone when you were talking to the guard, but he was obviously interested in you. He didn't stop looking through the blinds."

"I think it's good that I made him nervous."

"Maybe," she said.

"Just maybe?"

"That's all I can say about that right now."

"Why's that?"

"The guy in the black Camaro."

"What about him?"

"He's back there in traffic, following us."

Chapter 12

I kept with the flow, moving into the extreme left lane and stopping two cars short of the intersection at Semoran and Colonial a few minutes later.

The moment I switched lanes, the Camaro did the same, staying four vehicles behind us.

As I sat there, waiting for the light to change, Mike said, "Want me to drift back there and see what he's up to?"

"I'd appreciate a heads-up."

She was gone in a flash.

About three minutes later, the light finally changed. I followed the line turning left and headed west, toward downtown Orlando. I stayed in the extreme left lane, still considering my options. I wondered if I should make an abrupt left to try losing him. Not an option. The Camaro was a much lighter car and could easily outmaneuver the TransAm. It would be both foolish and extremely dangerous to try anything like that in this traffic. For all I knew, the guy in the Camaro could be a stunt driver. Or he could just be crazy. Either way, I'd lose.

Just then, I was forced to slow down when the traffic ahead of me slowly approached the next red light.

The moment I stopped, Mike reappeared in the seat next to me. "He's got a gun."

"I figured as much."

"He was on his cell phone, talking to that Johnston guy."

"Catch anything they were saying?"

"I moved in as close as I could and heard Johnston tell him they couldn't risk you riding around, asking questions."

"Did you find out who this guy is?"

"Johnston didn't call him by name."

"He didn't look familiar to you?"

"He's kind of grungy, with a five-day growth of beard. He's got tiny grease smears on his face and hands and is wearing a filthy sweatshirt and faded jeans. He looks like he might be a laborer. Or mechanic."

"Foreman Construction, maybe?"

"Possibly. You think he could have been hiding in the back seat of the Lexus in the ATM footage your rude police buddy showed you?"

"Anything's possible, I guess."

"You won't want to see him. Not up close, anyway."

"Why not?"

"He was screwing one of those muffler things onto his gun."

"A silencer?"

"Yes."

I went back to considering my options. The fact that a goon was trailing me and was armed with a gun and silencer made things much more frightening.

"What are you thinking?"

"I'm thinking that I might have to use my gun after all."

"Why? You still have me, you know."

"I know."

"Why don't you sound more confident, then?"

"There's a guy following me who has a gun."

"But you still have *me*…"

I didn't want to tell Mike that even though she'd saved my butt several times over the years, the fact that an armed man following me in heavy traffic still scared the piss out of me. It would probably hurt her feelings. So I said, "I still have to think my way out of this one," and hoped she'd understand.

"I think I understand."

"Really?"

"Sure. Even though we're a team, you're still your own man, right?"

"I've got to fight my own battles."

"I wouldn't respect you if you didn't."

"Thank you."

"So, what do you plan to do?"

"I think my best bet is to drive on over to Police Headquarters."

"Didn't your rude police buddy say he'd be leaving at around six?"

"I'm gonna gamble on the possibility that the psycho following us won't want to get anywhere near Police Headquarters."

"That sounds reasonable."

"First of all, silencers are illegal. Secondly, unless I'm mistaken, he probably has a record. If he's stopped, it could mean a prison sentence. I don't think he'd want to risk that."

"I'm glad you can think so logically in such a tense situation."

"Are you trying to butter me up for something?"

"I'm just trying to convince you that you show terrific resourcefulness under pressure."

"Thank you."

"There's a however in there I really don't want to bring up, but I know I have to."

"What the hell? Bring it on."

"Have you thought about what you'll do if you're wrong?"

"About what?"

"What if the man following us really is crazy and doesn't mind getting near Police Headquarters?"

"Then I guess I'm going to need *your* resourcefulness to fall back on."

***

It was around 8:15 when I pulled into the parking lot of Police Headquarters and parked the TransAm in an end space about two rows down from the rear entrance.

The lot was more than half-filled. Not exactly a good thing. Parked vehicles meant dynamite hiding places, especially for a psycho armed with a gun. However, the area was well-lit in several strategic positions. To make things even better, several uniformed cops were walking around, and nearly a dozen others in business suits were leaving and entering through the rear door. I hoped this would deter my assailant from targeting me. It might even encourage him to consider calling off his hunt entirely.

"Any sign of the Camaro?" I asked Mike.

"Let me slip away and look for him."

She vanished.

A few seconds later, I heard approaching footsteps.

"That you, Deacon?"

I turned.

A tall, lanky uniform was walking up to my side of the car. The moment I tried remembering the man's name, his nametag glinted in the reflection of one of the spots. *Donaldson*. Yes. Frank Donaldson. A sergeant, going by the three stripes. I'd seen him several times in Neil's office.

"Hi, Frank. How goes it?"

He nodded and began checking out the TransAm. I could spot a car guy a mile away. As much as I disliked male bonding, I appreciated it when someone noticed my car.

I also realized that if a bullet came at me, it would probably hit Donaldson. He was a big guy and made a substantial barrier.

I knew how that made me sound, but I wasn't quite ready to die yet.

"Flies, don't she?"

"Like a scalded cat."

"Don't make 'em like this anymore."

"Nope."

He shrugged. "Personally, I don't think I'll ever go with anything but power steering and brakes."

"I hear you."

"Original shocks on this baby?"

"I had them replaced a couple of years ago."

A nod. "That helps."

"Feeding her gets pricey, though. She loves her food."

"I can imagine." He straightened. "Seen Neil lately?"

"Earlier this morning. I'm helping out with the Sheffield case."

He thought for a moment. "The dead stripper?"

"That's the one."

"That's right. You were hauled in."

"It wasn't a great evening for me."

"Be glad you were cleared."

"I am, believe me."

"I heard Davenport and Gaffman were assigned to that one."

"I'm the key eyewitness, so…" I shrugged.

"That's why they hauled you in?"

"I was standing right there when you guys found her with her throat slit."

"How close?"

"About as close as you are to me."

"You didn't see what happened?"

I shrugged. I didn't think it would help if I told him too much.

He shook his head. "Weird."

"You got that right…"

Mike reappeared in the seat beside me. "He's sitting in his car at the end of the block, talking to that Johnston guy on his cell. His gun and silencer are on the seat beside him."

"Any leads yet?" Donaldson asked.

124

"Maybe. By the way…wanna tip on an armed felon?"

His eyes narrowed. "Howzat?"

"Don't know his name, but he's sitting in an older model black Camaro at the end of the block, and he's got a gun with a silencer sitting on the seat beside him."

He blinked and reached for his radio. "And ya know this how?"

"A very good friend just passed him. She called me just as I was pulling in."

"How good's this info?"

"As good as it gets."

"You're sure the perp's a felon?"

"Positive."

He began barking into his radio. Then he sprinted toward the rear of the building, where the line of cruisers sat in the front row.

I flicked on the ignition.

"Are we gonna get closer for a better seat?" Mike asked.

"We don't want to get in their way." I pulled out and took the car over to the entrance, which brought me back out onto the main drag. I went about half a block, then stopped when we had a clear view of the street ahead. I put the car in park, took my binoculars from the glove box, adjusted them, and rested my elbows on the steering wheel.

Using the other entrance, a cruiser, possibly the one carrying Donaldson, reached the end of the block. Its lights flashing, it pulled directly in front of the Camaro while another cruiser sped up the street, stopping twenty feet or so directly behind it.

A third cop car had pulled onto the street about a hundred feet on our right, blocking access.

His gun drawn, Donaldson got out of his car and cautiously approached the Camaro. The cop in the other cruiser had already opened his door. He stood behind it, crouched, his gun drawn as well. Moving closer, Donaldson lowered his piece. The other cop moved sideways. His gun still drawn, he approached the Camaro from behind. When he was about five feet from it, he holstered his weapon, grabbed his radio and spoke into it. Both cops opened the doors of the Camaro. Then, bending over, they began looking inside.

"I take it our guy's gone," I said.

No response.

I pulled my face away from the binoculars.

Mike had disappeared again.

"Mike?"

A moment later, she reappeared. "He's gone."

"I figured. I take it the cops are pissed."

"I wouldn't say that. They found a gun underneath the driver's seat. And the one you were talking to just called the Lab and told them they were bringing in a car to dust."

"I guess Donaldson believed what I told him."

"Apparently they're taking it very seriously. One of them spotted blood in the back seat."

***

Mike and I got back to my South Conway condo just before 9:00.

It was already dark, and I was tired. I wanted to relax with a splash of Jack Daniels, take a nice long shower and head off to bed.

126

And think. This case was getting scarier by the hour, and I was afraid that if I got any closer to solving it, I'd end up dead.

I knew I shouldn't be too worried about the guy in the black Camaro. He'd escaped the police, but since he probably didn't know where I lived, I shouldn't expect any more trouble from him for quite a while.

Somehow, that reasoning wasn't very reassuring.

The guard wasn't sitting on his stool in his little guard shack when I pulled into the complex. He was either making his rounds or enjoying a nap in his clunker, a thirty-year-old dirty gray van. It was equipped with a mattress in back and was always parked in front of the complex, less than fifty feet from his station. I didn't care where he was or what he was doing. I just eased on past and took the TransAm down the long straight stretch and around the back, where my condo overlooked the tennis court and the small lake a few hundred yards from the far northeastern side of the complex.

"You're sure you're not worried about that guy?" Mike asked as I parked in my designated spot. "The one in the black Camaro?"

"He has more urgent things to be concerned with." I didn't want Mike to know how I felt about all this. "If I were in his shoes, I'd be more worried about the Orlando Police hunting me down. They took his car, so he can't get around as easily. I'm the least of his problems."

"Still, you never know about these guys. They act stupid, but when it comes to finding people..." She shrugged.

"Once the cops dust his car, they'll find his prints. He's obviously got a record, so they'll be looking at him for murder and a bunch of other Class A felonies." I pulled out my keys and pushed open my door.

"Yes, but—"

I turned back to where she was sitting. "But what?"

All I saw was a look of total shock on her lovely face.

Before I could say anything else, something hard slammed into the back of my skull. Everything went black.

Chapter 13

I woke up in total darkness, the back of my head throbbing. Something had been shoved over my head and pulled down. I figured it was probably a pillowcase, or small sack.

After some painful experimentation, I realized that my arms were pulled behind my back and fastened together at the wrists and my legs were tied together at the ankles. I was lying on my right side, and my right arm had gone numb.

Gritting my teeth, I shifted my weight until I was lying on my stomach. The effort cost me considerably. A hot batch of other aches and pains scurried up my right side like ants escaping an open flame. My right arm, relieved of the extreme pressure, awakened—but not without cost. A cluster of bright pain exploded from my shoulder and a tingling sensation took over my right side.

As I lay there, struggling, I forced my brain to go back to what I was doing before everything went black. It took several moments, but I finally remembered.

Mike and I had just got back to the condo. The guard hadn't been at his post. I'd gone right on through.

Then, as I parked the TransAm in my designated spot, Mike said something.

What was it?

It took a while longer for my brain to start functioning again, but the conversation eventually came back.

"You're sure you're not worried about that guy?" she'd asked.

What guy was she talking about?

The blackness returned.

Once again, my memory took some time to start back up.

A guy in a black Camaro had been following us. He was somehow connected to the case I was working on. I'd shaken him by driving directly to Police Headquarters and...

Then what?

Once again, my memory dimmed.

Somehow, that didn't concern me right now. What mattered most was my present predicament. Someone had snuck up to me at the condo and whacked me in the back of the head. Unless the guard had been dozing off for quite a while, there was only one way someone could have snuck in and done the deed.

He had no doubt come in through the side entrance of the complex, where the privacy fence opened up to the rear lot of the strip mall behind my complex. He would have parked near the privacy fence in the mall lot, which was normally almost always empty at this time of night. Then he'd snuck onto our property and hidden behind one of the parked cars.

Since my spot was only half a dozen spaces from the gate, he wasn't far away. All he had to do was wait for me, sneak over, and whack me while I was getting out of the TransAm. He'd then dragged or carried me over to the gate, dumped me in the trunk of his vehicle and sped off.

Mike tried to warn me but obviously hadn't seen him in time.

However, none of that was relevant. I had other more important things to consider.

As softly as I could, I whispered, "Mike? Are you here?"

"Of course," she replied, her voice just inches away.

Relief swept through me. Suddenly I wasn't nearly as frightened. But I was still helpless, and there were still bad guys wandering around out there.

I had the feeling they weren't far away.

"Are we alone?"

"For now."

"What happened?"

"He was waiting for you."

"Where are we?"

"Somewhere on Semoran, south of Gatlin. This is a storage locker. The guy who suckered you is the same guy I saw in the black Camaro."

"Where is he?"

"He's not far. When he comes back, I recommend that you don't act like you know anything. He's nasty and sweaty and looks really angry. Act stupid and maybe he won't consider you a threat."

"That's not far from the truth."

"What isn't?"

"Not knowing anything. I'm getting some idea of what's happening, but I'm still sort of working blindly on this one."

131

"Well, act stupid anyway. You can do it. You're good at it. You even do it when you're not even trying."

"Gee, thanks."

"I'm trying to help. I obviously can't untie you, but I'll help in any other way I can."

"I guess he took my gun."

"Yes. He did."

"Damn. I liked that gun."

"You can get another one once you get out of this."

"I just hope I can."

"As I just said, I'll help."

"I appreciate you being here, you know..."

"If I were you, I'd stop whispering."

"Why?"

"I think he's coming back."

***

A heavy door not far from where I lay rolled open loudly, stopping briefly before banging closed.

Heavy footsteps approached me.

I lay there, frightened, not moving. Instinct—as well as professional memory—made me tense my stomach muscles just in case my new visitor wanted to display some instant sadistic superiority by kicking a helpless man in the midsection.

My fears were quickly proven wrong. Instead of kicking me, my captor straddled me. Rough hands grabbed my shoulders and pulled, forcing me to sit up. My right arm tingled even more, and my back thumped against something hard. I had no idea what it was. Mike must have sensed what I was thinking. She said, "You're leaning against a wooden crate."

I might have guessed it wouldn't be a soft cushion or mattress.

Whatever had been shoved onto my head was yanked off. Whoever grabbed it had also snatched a thick clump of my hair. It stung sharply, and I winced.

"Ow!"

"Quit bein' a baby," said a man in a low-pitched growl. A moment later, something soft dropped quietly on the concrete floor just a foot or so from my bound ankles. "Be glad that's not *all* I pulled."

I opened my eyes slowly and squinted.

Mike was right: this was a storage locker. It was a big one, too. About the size of a two-car garage, stacked with crates and boxes. The walls on my right and left were nearly covered up to the seven-foot-high ceiling. A pair of long fluorescent lights blipped in the center of the rafters in the ceiling, creating an eerie haze.

The man facing me was about five-ten, broad-shouldered and solidly built. He wore a loose-fitting lightweight maroon jacket over a filthy sweatshirt. He also wore faded jeans and smudged tennies. He had short black hair, and his face matched Mike's description of the guy following us on Semoran—grungy, with a five-day growth of beard and grease on his face and hands. My gut, plus the throbbing in the back of my skull, told me that this asshole wasn't going to make the next few minutes pleasant for me.

Just then, he took one step toward me, which brought him to within a foot of my bound ankles. "I'm gonna ask you a few questions," he growled. "I want answers, and I don't care what I gotta do to get 'em. Get it?"

I hesitated.

He immediately raised his right foot and brought it sharply back down onto my right kneecap.

The pain was unbearable. For a moment I thought a grenade had gone off in my knee. I cringed, gritting my teeth as a hot flash of blinding agony raced up my leg, stopping near my collarbone, shifting a little and settling warmly between my shoulder blades. The flash stayed bright for a few moments, ebbing finally, then settling into a distant throbbing.

I opened my eyes again. They were filled with tears. I noticed right off that he hadn't budged. Then, to my horror, I saw that he'd raised his right foot again. It rested about a foot above my kneecap, ready to come down again. In the same spot. "I *said*, get it?"

"I get it, dammit." My helplessness had quickly transformed into anger.

"Brute." Mike was definitely angry. I sincerely hoped she could do something while I was still able to walk.

"Good." He lowered his foot to the concrete floor and stepped back. "And watch the attitude, buddy. I'm the one callin' the shots."

"You don't want attitude? Then keep your sadistic tendencies in check."

"Watch it, I said." He stepped toward me again. "You really wanna say somethin' that'll piss me off?"

I knew better than continue, but I didn't want him to think this would be easy for him. Mike's presence helped immensely. "Let's just get on with it, okay?"

"You got balls." He nodded. "I like that."

I wanted to tell him that I could care less what he liked.

He watched me closely for another moment or two. "I got some questions I need answered. See, you seem to show up where you ain't s'posed to, and you also seem to know shit you shouldn't know about. In other words, you got certain folks all nervous and bothered, and they want me to find out what's goin' on. Get it?"

"Yeah. I get it."

"Good. You know why you're here, then. First question: how do you know what's goin' on?"

"Going on?"

He raised his foot again. "I ask, you answer. Get it?"

"Yeah, I get it."

"You really need to listen to him," Mike said, appearing hazily on my right. "He's crazy, and he's already hurt you."

"I know." I was relieved to see her right there beside me. I also hoped she could do something to bring this session of pain to an abrupt end. "Believe me."

My captor raised his head. "What?"

"I said—"

135

"I heard what ya said. I just wanna know why ya said it."

"I think this'll go much better if I stepped in," Mike said.

"I think you're right."

"Ya better believe I'm damn right…"

"I just said it, didn't I?"

His foot came up again. "Didn't we just agree that I ask the fuckin' questions?"

"I just agreed so you wouldn't smash my kneecap again."

"Ya know what, smartass?" His foot went up another two inches. "I've decided that I'm sick and tired of your shit."

"Maybe he's sick and tired of yours, too," Mike said.

She had obviously made her voice audible to him.

Startled by the sound, he turned around awkwardly, his foot slamming to the floor, dangerously close to my throbbing kneecap. It put him off-balance, and he almost fell. "What the fuck? Who…what's goin' *on*?"

Although he obviously couldn't see her, she stood about three feet away from him. "Why are you hurting my best friend? It's totally unnecessary, you know. He'll answer your questions if you just ask them, so stop acting like a sadistic psychopath."

Flustered, he backed up. His hand disappeared beneath the flap of his jacket. It came back out gripping a gun and silencer. "Who the hell…what the fuck's goin' on here?"

"I don't think your mother would approve," Mike said. "You do have a mother, don't you?"

Without hesitation, he pointed his gun in Mike's direction and popped off three quiet shots.

"That wasn't very friendly," she said. "You really don't know how to treat women, do you?"

"What the fuck *is* all this?" His hand shook. He pressed the trigger two more times. The slugs slammed into wooden crates, lodging deeply in them. "Who the hell…what the fuck *are* ya?"

"If I tell you, will you promise to stop shooting at me? It's extremely rude, you know."

He fired two more rounds into a large block of cut lumber sitting next to the wooden crates.

"I guess that answers my question," she said flatly.

"You…you're a *ghost*?"

"If I am, why do you keep shooting at me? Everyone knows about ghosts. You can't possibly hit us with anything. Not even bullets. Yours are sailing right through me. The only thing you're hitting is the stuff in this room. And just in case you haven't figured this out yet, we're not going to get anywhere if you keep this up."

"Shit. Damn. Fuck." Still shaking, he kept looking around, gawking.

"Your vocabulary really needs work," she said. "Did you ever go to school? Or did you forget everything they tried teaching you?"

"Man, this is so *totally fucked up*!" He suddenly shifted his position and turned the gun toward me.

I closed my eyes, turned my head away and began to pray.

"You really don't want to do that, you know…"

"Shit. This is…*shit*!" He pressed the trigger.

The gun did not fire.

"I told you not to do that," Mike said. "That's my friend. I don't want him dead or even slightly injured. And while we're on the subject, I didn't like it one bit when you stepped on his kneecap. That was a really nasty, ignorant thing to do. You can seriously hurt someone doing that. He's not a young man anymore. If you injure his kneecap, he'll have trouble walking for the rest of his life. You don't want *that*, do you? I know *I* don't…"

"Listen… Whoever—whatever you are…lady, ghost, whatever—I don't know what's goin' on."

Mike disappeared and reappeared just a few feet behind him. "Why do you keep looking over there? I'm over here."

He cringed, nearly dropping the gun.

Mike disappeared again and reappeared on his right, between him and the door. "Now I'm over here."

He spun around and put a slug through the door.

"*Now* look what you've done." She drifted over and stopped behind him. "There could be someone outside, walking past, and if there was, you might have just killed or seriously wounded—"

"Man, this is *really fucked up*!"

Mike turned to me. "What's wrong with this guy?"

"He's as dumb as a post."

"What the fuck…what's goin' on…who the fuck…"

"You really need to work on expanding your vocabulary," Mike said. "Your former teachers would be cringing in horror if they heard what's been coming out of your mouth."

He was no longer listening. He moved around awkwardly, stumbling, frantically scanning the room. Dropping the gun, he dashed over to the door, dropped to his knees, pulled it open about two feet and rolled outside.

Chapter 14

I gawked at the two-foot gap beneath the roll door in disbelief.

Expecting him to come back and finish the job. He didn't. The gap stayed empty. Then I turned to where Mike was still hovering above the floor just five or six feet away. "That was good, Mike. Thank you. You saved my ass again."

"No problem."

"The only thing I didn't really care for was that snide remark about my age."

Mike smiled. "It's true, isn't it? You're over forty now. In fact, you've been over forty for at least—"

"I know how long I've been over forty, thank you."

"I was about to say that, statistically speaking, you're no longer—"

"Forget about those damned statistics. The only thing I really care about right now is finding some way of cutting through these damned zip-ties."

"I wish I could help."

"I know."

"But I can't. We've been through this same thing before."

"I'm well aware of that, thanks."

"I only mentioned it because I feel guilty about not being able to help you."

"At least you saved my kneecaps."

"I had to get that man out of here. He's dangerous."

"You think?"

"Well, he hit you over the head, brought you here, tied you up and then tried to shatter your kneecap. Yes, he's dangerous."

"That, plus the fact that he showed definite signs of homicidal behavior when he began shooting blindly at a ghost. Then shot at a door leading to a road where other people could be walking past."

"I'm glad you could think professionally even though you were in a very helpless and vulnerable position."

"Lots and lots of training." I checked out the crate behind me, looking for sharp edges I could use to slice through the zip-ties.

"But at least he's gone now, and you still have your kneecap all in one piece."

"Well, yeah, but I still need to get the hell out of—"

"Sshhh…" She tilted her head and turned toward the door.

Light footsteps. My pulse hastened.

A pair of tennies and slim ankles covered in denim appeared in the two-foot-gap.

"It looks like you're about to have another visitor," Mike said.

A moment later, the door rolled up another two feet to show a slender, small-breasted young woman with long dark-brown hair. She bent beneath the roll door and came inside. She was about five-five and looked about twenty-three or so, with a pretty face and dark eyes staring at me behind a pair of large, thick-framed glasses. She nervously scanned the storage locker before taking another step.

141

Then I noticed the pocketknife in her right hand. It was opened, with the blade pointed straight at me.

"Mike?" I whispered nervously.

"I'm here. Don't worry."

The girl hurried toward me. Just as she reached me, she dropped to her knees and sliced through the zip-tie pinning my ankles together. It took me a moment to realize what she'd actually done. Then, without a word, she crawled closer and, pushing my right shoulder away from the crate, used the knife to free my wrists.

"Thank you." I rubbed my numb wrists, then my tingling arms. I couldn't believe my luck. "Who are you?"

She pressed an index finger to my lips. "*Sshhh!*" Her dark eyes narrowed and became enormous behind the glasses. She carefully closed her knife, shoved it in the rear pocket of her skintight jeans and straightened. "Can you stand?"

"I don't know yet. Give me a minute."

"Please hurry. We only have a minute or so before they come back."

They...

Were these the "certain folks" the kneecap-buster had mentioned? The people who were nervous and bothered because I kept showing up when and where I wasn't supposed to show up?

Time to sort that out later.

I had no idea who this girl was or what part she played in this. I figured that since she'd just freed me, I should trust her—at least for right now. I also

142

decided that she knew what she was talking about. Besides, I had no other option at the moment.

Gritting my teeth, I grabbed a corner of the wooden crate to support my weight. The girl gripped my left arm and helped me straighten. Holding my breath and concentrating on ignoring the pain and weakness in my legs and kneecap, I let her help me outside.

***

Spotlights bolted to the roofs of the long line of storage buildings sprayed the darkness with a soft film of hazy white.

I had no idea where we were, but at this point, it didn't matter. I cared only about my numb legs, my throbbing joints and the hot pain in my kneecap and hoped my condition wouldn't hinder my escape. I let the girl help me down the narrow alley between buildings, where a late-model Honda Accord awaited us at the far end.

"Who *are* you?" I was really curious about this young woman and why she'd just freed me. And, most of all, why she'd shown up when she did.

"Later," she whispered, pulling me along. "There's no time for talk right now."

I decided to let her run the show. I cared only that she'd freed me and gotten me out of there before the psycho had a chance to recover from his shock and come back to finish me off.

Once we reached the Honda, she helped me into the passenger seat and closed the door. While I situated myself in the seat, she circled the front of the car and got in behind the wheel. Mike's hazy form materialized directly behind me as the girl started up the ignition. Then, without flicking on her lights, she slammed it into reverse and backed up quickly.

"Why are we backing up?" I asked.

"Guess." She pointed at the windshield.

Straight ahead, the glare from flashing headlights announcing an approaching vehicle lit up the road.

The girl backed up all the way to the rear of the facility, put the car in gear and went down the opposite way, until the front entrance came into view. Without slowing down, she shot through the front gate and pulled out recklessly into a small hole in traffic.

We were heading north on Semoran Boulevard in a flash.

I turned around in my seat. Aside from heavy traffic, I saw no sudden explosion of headlights emerging from the storage facility, nor anyone approaching the front gate.

I turned back to the girl. "What's this all about? Who are you? Since we're obviously a fairly safe distance away, I think it's safe to talk to me now."

She kept with the northward flow, swerving from one lane to the next when the opportunity arose, all the while keeping a sharp lookout in her rearview mirror.

"I'm Lisa Randolph."

"Hello, Lisa. I'm—"

"I know who you are."

"Really? Who am I?"

"You don't know who you are?"

144

"I know who I am. I'd like to know who you *think* I am."

"If you've got a bastard like Reid Johnston after you, I assume you're either a private detective or someone being paid by one of his enemies to take him down."

This didn't surprise me. It could have been the truth or just something she might have figured out on her own. But it also told me she was somehow involved in this.

"You really need to find out how she knows all this," Mike said from the back. "Something's very wrong."

Mike was absolutely right.

"How do you know all this?" I asked.

"I'm his stepdaughter."

"Whose stepdaughter?"

"Johnston's."

"Really?"

"That's what I just said, didn't I?"

"I'm finding this hard to believe."

"Why would I say such a thing if it wasn't true?"

"I didn't know Johnston was married."

"How could I be his stepdaughter if he wasn't married?"

"That's a pretty valid point."

"What's the problem, then?"

"I'm just finding it difficult to believe that the man's married when he's been seen—very recently, I might add—in the company of strippers."

145

"Just one stripper, and her name was Dusty Rhodes. Anyway, the bitch is dead now, so why is that an issue?"

Her tone was extremely disturbing. I was also getting something else that I couldn't quite put my finger on. Since I had to know what was going on, I had to use my proven technique of asking irritating questions. My technique didn't make me any friends, but it almost always got my questions answered.

"It's not," I told her.

"Then let's please get off the subject."

"Which one? The stripper? Or your stepfather?"

"I'd rather not talk about either of them, if you don't mind."

"I take it you don't like the man."

A deep sigh. "Just in case you haven't already been able to figure it out by now, I hate the bastard."

"I think I got that, but thanks for clearing it up."

"Then why are you still talking about it when I asked you not to?"

"It's a bad habit I've picked up over the years."

"I'm sure you've got more than one."

"Ouch," Mike said.

"I take it family holidays are not quite festive for you anymore."

She didn't reply.

"You're not Facebook buddies either, are you?"

"Look, I'm his stepdaughter, not his daughter. My mother married him a couple of years ago. She didn't ask me how I felt when she was shacking up

146

with the bastard and didn't ask me how I felt after she'd married him." She shot me a seething glare. "No, I don't spend much time at all with her anymore. And just in case you couldn't figure this one out yourself, he's not on my Facebook page. Neither is my mother."

"Sorry to hear that."

She shrugged. "It's no biggie. I'm okay with it now."

"Really?"

"It helps a lot when the person you hate doesn't give a rat's ass if you live or die."

"Something's not quite right," Mike said. "I'm picking up some vibes that don't exactly go with her story."

The girl's story made sense, but I trusted Mike's intuition and figured something just didn't add up. Mike could be totally right, but even so, I couldn't put my finger on any of this. Right now, I had mixed feelings about the whole thing. This girl had just saved my life. I realized that this fact alone could be swaying my opinion a tad. Even so, my professional instinct told me something else was going on. Something that I needed desperately to figure out.

"You're sure about that?" I asked Mike.

"I'm sure," Mike said.

The girl glared at me again. "Why'd you say that? Of course I'm sure."

Since I couldn't remember what I'd just said, I had to bluff my way through this. "I'm a private eye. I say a lot of things. Sometimes I say stuff that doesn't make sense just so the person I'm talking to can argue about it and give me something else to work with. Other times I'll say something that makes it seem like I haven't been paying attention. But I was actually paying attention and just said it to make the other person lower his guard and reveal something they didn't want me to know."

She didn't reply.

We passed La Costa Drive as well as Lido Street. This told me we hadn't been far away from Johnston's land investment office south of Gatlin.

I decided to move on to more crucial issues.

"Why'd you save my ass back there?"

Once again, she shot me an angry glance. "It seemed the right thing to do at the time."

"Well, thanks for doing it, all the same."

"You're welcome."

"You need to find out more about that," Mike said.

"I know."

"Why did you say that?" Lisa Randolph asked.

"Say what?"

"I know."

"You know what?"

She groaned. "I realize I've already told you this before, but do you know just how irritating you are?"

"I consider it one of my best qualities."

"Well, quit doing it. It's pissing me off."

"I know."

She sighed and pushed some hair roughly away from her face.

"Let's start all over again, okay?"

"Whatever."

148

"First of all, how did you show up when you did?"

"I was out there and saw him."

"Out where?"

"The storage locker, silly. Where else?"

"How did you know I was even in there with him?"

"I didn't."

"Then how did all this happen?"

"I saw him drive by when I was taking stuff out of my locker."

"You have a locker?"

"Of course I have a locker. Why would I be out there, taking things out of it if I didn't have one?"

"Touché."

"Now try asking me something that isn't stupid, okay?"

"I'll try. Then you recognized the man's car?"

"I see it all the time."

"Where?"

"At my stepfather's business. And he's been to the house a couple of times."

This was beginning to sound too pat. "I take it they're friends, then?"

"That idiot's a goon my stepdad uses from time to time. I always steer clear of him because he makes me want to take a shower every time I see him. The way he stares at me…" She shivered.

"I can understand that," Mike said.

"I have a small locker where I keep my stuff just down the aisle from my stepfather's. Where you were. When I saw him show up and open his trunk,

149

I knew he was up to something, so I ducked out of sight."

"Then you were watching him when he dragged me in there?"

"How else could I have known about you?"

That made sense.

"Is that all you wanted to know? Or do you still think there's something strange about me?"

"You can tell me why you saved my ass. The real reason this time. And then tell me what's going on back there. Maybe we can try and get along a little better."

"That bastard's involved in a lot of bad stuff."

"Which bastard are we talking about now?"

"Which bastard do you think?"

"Well, the jerk who makes you want to have a shower obviously qualifies, so let's start with him."

"What was he doing to you?"

"He seemed to have a slightly unhealthy interest in shattering one of my kneecaps."

"That sounds like something he'd want to do."

"Well, that qualifies him as a psychotic as well as a bastard. At least, it does in my book."

She didn't reply.

"Who is he?"

"I don't know his name, but he really doesn't matter."

"Well, considering the fact that I only have two kneecaps and he was doing his best to destroy one or possibly both of them, I have to disagree. He really does matter. To me, anyway."

"In case you haven't already figured it out, he works at my stepfather's construction company and

150

does odd jobs whenever something dirty needs to be done."

"Such as kidnapping one of Orlando's finest private eyes, taking him to a storage facility and threatening to cripple him if he doesn't answer certain questions?"

She was quiet for a few moments. "Why'd he stop?"

"Stop what?"

"Hurting you. Why was he even doing that?"

"He said he wanted answers."

"Did you give him any?"

"I was about to, but he kind of got scared at the last minute and ran away."

She nodded. "Sounds like him. He spooks easily."

"He does that a lot?"

"Run away?"

"Let's go with that."

"Guy's a freak and a pervert. And seriously weird. I wouldn't put anything past him. I'm not quite sure why he just split during a dirty job, but that doesn't matter now, does it? You made out, didn't you?"

I nodded. "He's got a record, doesn't he?"

"What do *you* think?"

"I think he's got a record."

She shot me another quick glare. "You're really good."

"I can usually tell when someone's a criminal."

"How?"

"Well, one big clue is that law-biding citizens don't usually have the overwhelming urge to shatter

151

someone's kneecap. And they certainly don't hit someone over the back of the head, stuff them in the trunk of their car, take them to a storage facility, dump them on the floor and zip-tie them."

"You really *are* good."

"Save the accolades for later, after I can get home, have a drink, take a shower and get into my formal dinner jacket. Tell me more about your stepfather."

"Like what?"

"Let's start with his construction company."

"Well, for one thing, it isn't really a construction company."

"What is it, then?"

"He keeps construction supplies and equipment out there for show, but it's really nothing he needs to make big money."

"How does he make his money, then?"

"He deals with these people who bring in shipments of drugs. He keeps the drugs in storage at his construction company until the people come for them."

"You're saying his company is actually a stash house?"

"All I know is that the people who bring in the stuff pay him, and the people who come to pick it up pay him, too."

"Sounds like that could be pretty profitable."

"He weighs everything when it comes in. He gets so much a pound. He's making a fortune."

"Why are you telling me all this?"

"He's crazy, and he gets people killed. I'm sick of it."

152

Something about this still didn't sound legit.

"That's what all this is about? You don't like your stepfather? Or you don't like what he's doing?"

"I hate him and I hate what he does. Does that make sense?"

"Since I was obviously on the receiving end of one of his business ventures, I'd say it makes a lot of sense."

"For a minute I was afraid you didn't appreciate what I did."

"I appreciate what you did, all right. But it doesn't explain why you risked your life to help me escape."

"I thought I just did."

"You told me you hate your stepfather."

"How would you like it if your stepfather went around, having people killed and making big money from it?"

"I wouldn't like it much at all."

"All right, then."

"What's your mom think of all this?"

"She tried leaving him a couple of times, but he just sends people after her and they bring her right back."

"What does he think about you?"

"He knows how I feel about him. That's why I'm leaving."

"Really?"

"I've got all my stuff packed and I'm leaving early tomorrow morning. I've got a different car I bought under a different name. I'm keeping it in a parking lot on Colonial until I need it. I'd like to get to it early tomorrow morning, but I need a place to stay for the night so I can get some sleep."

"What's wrong with a motel?"

"I don't trust him. He's as smart as a fox. I know he suspects what I'm doing. If I'm right, he'll send out a couple of his boys and they'll check the motels to see if I'm staying there. I'm taking a big risk using this car. He already knows about it."

"Ask her why he even cares about her getting away," Mike suggested.

"Didn't you just tell me he doesn't care about you?" I asked.

"That's right."

"Then why would he go to all these great lengths to find you and—"

"He wants me dead."

"Why? Because you got me out of there?"

"I've been a thorn in his side ever since he married my mother. Besides, I'm sure that goon will go back there and figure it was me who got you out of the storage facility. That won't set well with him at all."

"How would he know?"

"My car was parked in plain view. I'm sure he's not *that* stupid."

"I don't know about this," Mike said.

Mike was right. There was something about this story that just wasn't adding up, but I couldn't put my finger on it. I kept remembering Neil telling me that Johnston had been in trouble a few times, but it had all been small stuff. I just couldn't see someone branching out from a couple of DUIs and a bogus embezzlement charge and operating a full-blown stash house drug exchange operation.

"Well?" she asked. "Will you help me get away?"

"That's why you helped me back there? So I'd help you?"

She shrugged. "I can't trust anyone else."

"Now she sounds pitiful," Mike said. "This really makes me suspicious."

"You're right," I told Mike.

"I'm glad you agree," Lisa Randolph said. "So…will you help me?"

"What do you want me to do?"

"Like I said, I've got to switch cars. I need to take you back to your place so you can use your car to follow me somewhere to dump this one. Then take me to my other car so I can get my stuff. I have to spend the night in a motel and get some sleep. Then I'll need a ride to the airport early in the morning so I can get on my plane. My real father lives in Washington State. I haven't seen him in years, and I miss him. We always got along."

I was silent, trying to digest all that.

"Well? Will you help me?"

"You'll never solve this case if you don't help her," Mike said.

I nodded.

"Does that mean you'll help me?"

"I owe you. Yeah, I'll help you."

"I appreciate it."

"Just don't turn your back on her," Mike said.

"I know," I said.

Lisa nodded.

Chapter 15

After Lisa Randolph turned into my condominium complex, we sat there while the guard staggered over to give us his customary nonsense.

"Live here, young lady?" He bent, squinting at Lisa and adjusting his glasses higher up on his nose. "Don't recall seein' ya before."

"I'm dropping off someone."

"Howzat?"

"She's an old friend," I told him.

He moved closer to the open window, squinted at me, and blinked. "Who's in there?"

"Guess."

He continued squinting. Then he blinked a few more times. "Ah… Didn't see ya at first."

"I tend to grow on people."

"Howzat?"

"Don't confuse him," Mike said behind me. "We'll be sitting here for half an hour while he tries to figure out what you just said."

I sighed. "Never mind."

"Can we go now?" Lisa asked.

The old man examined his wristwatch. "You're up kinda late, young lady. It's past eleven."

She glanced at me and frowned.

"You're making it even later," I said.

"Howzat?"

"We can't go to bed while you're standing here, keeping us both up."

"Huh? Oh. Yeah. Sorry." He thought that one over. Then, scowling in confusion, he straightened and gave us the go-ahead with his left arm while scratching the back of his neck with his right.

Lisa took the Honda down the one-way road. "Does he do that to you all the time?"

"Only when he's awake."

"That last thing you said. You weren't serious, were ya?"

"I like to confuse him. It gives him character."

"Is that why you've been confusing me?"

"You tell *me*."

She sighed. "Let's just stop this while you're still behind."

"Smart girl," Mike said.

Lisa stopped in front of my condo while I got into the TransAm. I really wanted to dash into my place and get another gun, but I didn't want to ruin this. The girl was in a hurry. I didn't know if she'd put up with any sort of delay. And if I came back outside and found her gone, I wouldn't have any idea where she'd gone.

As she crept away, I backed out of my spot and followed her back out and onto South Conway while the guard, still scratching the back of his neck, watched us.

Traffic was extremely light. We pulled out easily and headed south.

A couple of miles later, we turned into the strip mall facing Hoffner. Lisa took the Honda over to the far end of the lot and parked in front of the Chinese restaurant. Then she got out, hurried over to the TransAm and slipped into the seat beside me.

"Now where?" I asked.

"East Colonial."

I pulled back onto South Conway, and we headed north.

***

It was past midnight by the time we reached the Hyatt Regency at Orlando International.

Lisa's luggage consisted of two large, heavy gray Samsonite suitcases. Carrying them both, I followed her inside the huge, brightly lit hotel lobby and waited while she paid for a single room. She was carrying a small overnight bag as well as her large leather handbag and shuffled over to the elevators with her head down, obviously exhausted. As I watched her, I decided not to quibble about handling her luggage. She'd had a long, rough day. And since she'd helped me escape that storage locker before I was killed or seriously injured, I figured I owed her.

"Remember what I said about watching your back," Mike said as she followed us into the comfortable, air-conditioned single room. "I'm getting more and more negative vibes about all this."

So was I, since this brought back a similar memory. A few years earlier, while doing an errand for my ex-wife Phil, I'd carried an extremely heavy bag for a young female from the airport. It turned out that I'd been lugging around half a dozen pairs of light vinyl-covered dumbbells containing dozens of small packets of cocaine stuffed inside them.

Although I couldn't help thinking about that incident, I realized I was being foolish. Just because I was hauling around two heavy suitcases didn't mean this girl was hauling around cocaine-laced

158

dumbbells. And it certainly didn't mean this girl, who'd saved my life, was anything like the spoiled brat in that other case...

However, too many things about this case just didn't add up.

Although she'd given me a good explanation of why she'd shown up in the storage locker when she had, it still didn't make sense to me. It was too pat. Too convenient. And reeked too much of the cavalry-coming-in-at-the-perfect-time. Not to mention her story about Reid Johnston, which didn't sit very well with me right now.

She closed the door behind me and gestured to the luggage. "Just leave them over there, thanks." She pointed to the area in front of the end table next to the bed.

I set them down, straightened, and shook my hands to get the blood flowing in them again. "What do you have in there, by the way?" I asked casually. "Dumbbells?"

She shrugged. "All my personal stuff. I had most of my things in my storage locker until yesterday, when I put them in the rental. I was picking up the rest just as you were being brought in. I'm not coming back, so I've got to take everything I've got."

"Good point." Yep. It all sounded too convenient. Too pat.

"Wouldn't *you* take all *your* stuff if *you* were leaving a place forever?"

"What's next?" I decided to get off this subject as quickly as possible and find out what else she had in mind.

159

"My flight's not until noon. Actually, it's twelve-fifteen. Can you come back and get me at ten-thirty? They want me to be there an hour early."

"Sure."

"I'd ask you to stay with me, but..." She looked sheepish. "You know."

"Yeah. I know."

"There's only one bed, and...and, well, I can't ask you to sleep on the floor."

"I get it." I glanced at Mike. She was standing beside the bed, staring at the suitcases.

Lisa smiled briefly. The tiniest dimple on her left cheek appeared for an instant then disappeared.

Just as something else began nagging at me, she said, "If you like, I'll call you at your place around nine to see if you're up."

"That'll work." I pulled out my wallet, sorted through it and handed her one of my cards. "My home number's on it."

"Thanks again."

"No problem." I turned and left the room.

I went back outside and got into my car. For the next few minutes, I sat there and thought about the girl's smile. Just when I thought something was coming to me, Mike appeared beside me. There was a grim expression on her face.

"What is it?"

"You'll never guess what she's got in those suitcases."

"Dumbbells filled with cocaine?"

"Even better than that. Money. Lots of it."

"How much is lots?"

"Bundles. There are stacks of hundreds. I couldn't count it exactly because she's got it bundled and covered in newspapers, but going by the size of the area, I'd say she's carrying around close to half a million in those suitcases."

"Newspapers?"

"That's all I saw in there. Newspapers and money."

Chapter 16

Instead of driving back home, I stayed at the hotel and phoned Davenport.

"What the hell's goin' on, Deacon?" Davenport asked groggily. "It's what? One o'clock in the fuckin' morning!"

"To be precise, it twenty *past* one, but who's counting?"

"Deacon, dammit—"

"You want to solve this case or what?"

"What the hell are you talkin' about?"

"I thought the question was pretty clear. I'm watching the girl. She's here at the Hyatt Regency at the airport, but I have a strong feeling she won't be here much longer. All you and your partner have to do is get right over here and—"

"What girl?"

"She says she's Johnston's stepdaughter. "

"Deacon, you're not even s'posed to be on this case…"

"Listen to me—"

"If it hadn't been for Chief Haversack, your ass would still be—"

"I know, I know." He was beginning to make me wonder what I was even bothering to help him.

"You were caught standing at the scene—"

"Stay with me here, okay? You might just solve this case."

A pause, followed by a huge sigh. "All right. Whaddya got?"

"As I just told you, this girl says she's Johnston's stepdaughter."

Another pause, this one longer. "Johnston has a stepdaughter?"

"That's what she told me, but I'm pretty sure she's been lying to me about everything. I can usually tell when someone's lying to me."

"Johnston doesn't have a stepdaughter."

"You're sure?"

"Johnston's not even married right now. He's been married twice. His last divorce was finalized three years ago."

For some reason, I hadn't counted on that, but I knew better than voice my opinion—especially to an arrogant asshole like Davenport. "That really doesn't surprise me."

"So just who the hell *is* this so-called stepdaughter?"

"She told me her name is Randolph. Lisa Randolph. She's a brunette, about five-five, wears glasses—"

"They're not real," Mike said.

"What?"

Mike shrugged. "I peeked. Their lenses are clear glass."

"You're sure?"

Mike nodded.

"Damn..." I hated when someone duped me. Especially a female who helped me get away from a dangerous bad guy.

"Deacon, who the hell are you talkin' to?"

"A very close friend. Listen, if you want to solve this case, just come out to the Hyatt Regency.

You'll be able to see me as soon as you pull in. The girl—whoever she is—is staying here in the hotel. I brought her out here. And unless I miss my guess, she'll be calling for a cab very shortly. So I suggest you and Gaffman get here, ASAP."

"That it?"

"Just in case she slips past me, she told me she'll be on a flight to somewhere in Washington State. She also told me her flight's at twelve-fifteen, but as I just told you, I'm pretty sure she's been lying to me."

"Where the hell in Washington state?"

"If I knew, I'd damned sure tell you."

"Why tell us somethin' like that if she's been lyin' to ya?"

I took a breath and struggled to keep from calling him an asshole. Calling him that would make me feel better, but it would cause a bunch of complications I didn't need right now. "Let's just say I'm a good citizen and like to cooperate with the cops."

"By the way, I hate to remind ya once again, but you're not even s'posed to be workin' this case."

"You told me that before."

"Then why the hell do ya keep stickin' your nose where it doesn't belong?"

"Because you and your partner are taking entirely too damned long to solve it."

Davenport started to say something else, but I didn't want to hear any more of his bullshit. I hung up and pocketed the cell. Then I turned to Mike.

164

"You wonder how these cases manage to get solved at all, don't you?"

"I can understand why you don't like working with them," she said.

"Sometimes I think it's all in my imagination. Then all I have to do to convince myself otherwise is work with them on a case for a few hours. Then it all comes back."

"Right now, we have a much bigger problem."

"What's that?"

"I just drifted up there a minute ago and peeked in her hotel room."

"Keep going."

"You're not gonna like this…"

"Try me."

"The room's empty. She's already gone."

***

Davenport and Gaffman showed up at the Hyatt Regency about half an hour later, in an unmarked car followed by a police cruiser.

Davenport, his suit rumpled and his tie crooked, trudged over to the far end of the parking lot, where I was parked. Even his brush cut looked raggedly, somehow. I was standing beside my car, watching him as he approached. Gaffman remained in the passenger seat, talking to his cell. The uniform got out of the cruiser and stood in front of it, watching the hotel. I knew what I was about to tell Davenport would not make him happy. However, I'd worked with cops before. It didn't matter what you told them. Whatever it was, it didn't make them happy. I always thought it was the bad coffee they drank all day. Their constant heavy caseload didn't help, either.

Davenport flicked his stub of a cigarette toward the building. "What's goin' on?"

I ignored the stench of cigarette smoke and dragon breath emanating from him. That sort of stuff was soon going to be the least of my worries. "The girl's gone."

His bulldog face crinkled up. "I guess I'm not surprised."

I shrugged and tried to look apologetic, but my heart wasn't in it, and I probably ended up looking disgusted, instead. "I didn't think she'd slip away so soon."

He turned toward the building and grabbed his cell. "Ya didn't see anything?"

"She didn't come out, if that's what you mean."

"Then she's still in the building?"

"I honestly don't think so."

"Then how do ya know for sure?"

"Call it intuition."

Davenport didn't say anything for the longest time. Then he shook his head slowly and looked like he'd just tasted something that had just made him sick. "Ya know, if the Chief hadn't vouched for you, I'd be wonderin' what the fuck's goin' on with you."

"Neil's been wondering about me ever since we've known one another."

Davenport held on to his sour look. "Yeah. Whatever. I'd better go on over there and tell Gaffman what's goin' on. We could only bring one uniform out here, so we're basically on our own

166

here. By the way, we checked the flights on our way over."

"Let me guess. No noon flights to Washington State?"

"A couple to Seattle, but one takes off at two in the afternoon, the other at five in the evening."

I was beginning to feel like the world's biggest stooge. "Let me know when you plan on going in."

"Why would I wanna do that?"

"If you don't mind, I'd like to go in with you."

"I prefer ya stay right here."

"I know this is your case and all, but I still have a stake in this. After all, I was the only eyewitness to the Rhodes murder. And in case you haven't figured this out by now, I was set up to take the fall." I sincerely hoped I wouldn't have to say please. The thought of it made my stomach turn.

"Yeah. Whatever." Davenport must have felt a little something in my explanation. After a slight shrug, he shuffled back to his vehicle.

"I don't think he likes me," I told Mike.

"He has no taste."

Davenport went over to the car and began talking to Gaffman. The uniform walked over and stood beside Davenport. Then he and Davenport spun around and frowned at me.

"This doesn't look good," Mike said.

"It looks bad even for a guy as ugly as Davenport."

A moment later, Davenport spun on his heel and marched toward me. He didn't look pleased. "Just got the call," he said. "They found Johnston dead in his Winter Park condo."

"Murdered?"

"Throat was cut."

"I'll bet he's been dead a while," Mike said.

"How long?" I asked Davenport.

"A while."

"You're good," I whispered to Mike.

She smiled. "I get around."

"Save the compliments for someone who actually gives a shit," Davenport said.

Chapter 17

A few minutes later, Mike and I, trailing Davenport, Gaffman, the cop with them and the hotel night manager, snuck down the carpeted corridor.

The manager was young, about twenty-five, tall and skinny and as nervous as a cat as he held out his key card in front of him like some sort of defensive weapon. He swiped it and immediately sprinted to the end of the corridor, disappearing down the steps in seconds.

Except for the two large suitcases lying wide-open on the bed, the room was empty.

Gaffman pocketed his piece, put on his white gloves and began sorting through the contents of the suitcases.

"Anything?" Davenport asked.

"Not much." Gaffman shook his head. "Just a pair of old scuffed jeans and a pullover. A pair of glasses." He picked them up and squinted at them. "They're clear." He dropped them onto the jeans, picked up the crop top and dropped it on top of the jeans. "Hello…" He held up a dark-brown wig.

The moment I saw it, I felt the blood turn to ice in my veins.

Gaffman dropped it onto the crop top. "A disguise, obviously. We'll get the lab guys to pull some prints once we get them out here."

"She changed clothes," Mike said.

"Among other things," I said, trying to contain my anger.

"Whaddya babblin' about now?" Davenport was glaring again.

"That's the outfit she was wearing when she saved my life back at the storage facility on Semoran."

"She what?"

"Be right back," Mike said, and vanished.

"Johnston's guy suckered me back at my condo. He brought me out there. The girl told me she didn't know his name, but like everything else she said, it was probably a lie. Whoever he is, he no doubt worked for Johnston and obviously did some odd jobs for the guy. Lisa Randolph gave me the impression he was the one who slit the girl's throat outside Sheffield's, but now I'm not so sure."

"We ran across a name when we started on Johnston. Gillespie. Kevin Gillespie. He's got a sheet. His name came up when we brought in a black Camaro yesterday, about a block from the Station. Blood stains were found in the back seat."

"Whose blood?"

"The stripper found at Sheffield's." Davenport began frowning again. "Someone said you had somethin' to do with that."

"The dead stripper?"

Davenport groaned. "The Camaro bein' brought in."

"He'd been following me."

"This have anything to do with Johnston?"

"The girl told me this guy worked for Johnston. But as I just said, she's not known for her honesty."

Mike appeared in the doorway. "I found her."

I gave her a slight nod.

170

"I think I might know where the girl went," I said.

Both Davenport and Gaffman turned and gave me a couple of clueless expressions. The cop quickly joined in, but his scowl was more an expression of genuine curiosity. I figured he hadn't been a cop very long.

"Lemme guess," Davenport said sourly. "She ain't here, is she?"

Mike remained in the doorway, gesturing to her right.

"No, but I have this feeling."

"The first floor," Mike said.

"She's on the first floor," I finished.

"And ya know this how?" Davenport asked.

"I'll tell you all about it later." I rushed for the doorway and followed Mike down the balcony, toward the end, where the iron staircase awaited us both.

***

Although it was nearly three o'clock, hotel activity was fairly high.

Guests coming in and leaving provided a constant flow that clogged the elevators as well as the halls and corridors. Baggage carts and dollies filled with luggage and racks of garment bags served as obstacles cluttering the walkway. Porters and hostesses scurried in all directions, dodging guests as they tended to their individual tasks. Bar patrons staggered around, getting in everyone's way.

171

I followed Mike down the walkway, dodging bleary-eyed travelers sleepwalking to their rooms. "Now what?" I whispered when the coast was clear.

"Not much farther," she said, moving in a straight line as she passed through slow-moving clots of travelers following the porters and baggage handlers.

We turned the corner and went down another walkway, which led to another wing of rooms.

At the end of the corridor, a slender figure moved quickly, hauling a large crate on wheels behind her. She was heading straight for the exit, which led to the side parking lot.

"That's her," Mike said.

"Are you sure?"

Mike gave me one of her looks.

"Did you get a good look at her?"

"Yes. And it's her."

"I'm only asking because she only had two suitcases, and she left both of them in her room."

"She obviously had that crate stashed somewhere else, silly. She's most likely been planning this for a while."

"Maybe, but there's still something not quite right about this."

"Trust me. That's Lisa Randolph. The girl who rescued you at the storage locker. And I'll also wager that she's your blond goddess."

"Something's been bugging me for quite a while. It's probably the height thing that rubbed me the wrong way. Lisa Randolph is about five-four, maybe five-five. The blonde who approached me at Sheffield's was my height."

172

"She was probably wearing super high heels when you first saw her. That would make her anywhere between four and six inches taller."

"You're right. The blond wig and clothes added to the disguise. Thanks for the input, Mike."

"Something tells me you already knew Lisa Randolph was your girl."

"It was that dimple in her left cheek," I said. "No two people have the same smile. When she smiled at me in the hotel room, I knew I'd seen that smile before. And when you told me the glasses were fake, I was convinced. Lisa Randolph is actually the tall blonde we've been looking for."

"We're both right, but the hard part has yet to come."

"The hard part?"

"You've got to catch her without getting hurt."

"That's why I've got you, right?"

"Exactly."

"Excuse me!" I yelled after her.

The figure didn't stop, pause, or even turn around.

Mike and I kept moving toward her. When we were about ten feet away, I said, "We know what's going on, Lisa. Or whatever your real name is."

The figure still did not acknowledge us.

I hurried up the last few yards, until I was right beside her. Then I grabbed her cart by the strap, stopping it and nearly knocking her off-balance. She pulled away, backed up and glared. Then she lunged into a tirade of angry fluent Spanish. I didn't know much Spanish, but I could tell I was being cussed at.

Mike said, "It's her, all right."

173

I shot Mike a quick glance.

"Look at her. Forget the Spanish. Can't you tell this is her?"

Although it was semi-dark in the walkway, I could make out her features. This girl was definitely Lisa Randolph, but the eyes were different. Her coal-black hair was pulled back and tied in a tight ponytail starting at the crown of her head and nearly reaching her waist. She was wearing heavy makeup to make her look Hispanic. Her almond-shaped eyes seemed much larger, and her cheekbones were large and round. In her short black skirt and sleeveless red V-necked tee shirt, I could see her slight cleavage and small round breasts.

"Where you going, Lisa?"

She shrugged and looked uncomfortable. "*No comprendo.*"

I knew better than try and continue this with her in Spanish. It was ridiculous because I knew who she was, and she knew that I knew. Even if I tried going the Spanish route, nothing good would come of it. I'd end up saying something stupid.

But I had to do something to force her to reveal who she actually was.

"Talk to her." Mike was obviously thinking the same thing I was. "Tell her something she needs to know."

I knew where Mike was going but still had no idea how to proceed.

"Tell her she lied to you."

That was all I needed. "You lied to me, didn't you?"

Her dark brows bumped together. "*Que?*"

"You said your flight was at noon. There *is* no flight, is there?"

She just shrugged.

"If I were you, I'd start talking. In English, this time. In less than a minute, three Orlando cops will be showing up here. When they see you, I won't be able to do anything to help you out of this—"

"No comprendo…"

I tried one last gamble. "I'll say this, though. You're really good with those disguises. I'd never guessed you're the same girl who approached me at Sheffield's with that sob story about someone following you, when all the while you had Dusty Rhodes all decked out in the back seat of her Lexus with her throat cut. Did you do the deed? Or was it that Gillespie flunky you were leading around by his—"

Like lightning, Lisa buried her left arm in the side pocket of her handbag. It came back out an instant later holding a gun and silencer. Just before she brought it in front of her, Mike materialized on my left and said, "I wouldn't use that thing if I were you…"

Startled by Mike's voice, Lisa turned sharply and got off a round that thumped against the brick wall. It ricocheted. An instant later, I felt a piercing hot stabbing punch in my right side, just below the ribs. Despite the immediate onslaught of agonizing pain, I dove for the gun. At that same moment, Lisa shifted, her left side pushing me away. The gun went off again, missing my face by inches. Another slug slapped into the wall behind us again, and I gritted my teeth as I waited for the second ricochet

175

to hit me. Instead, it slapped into the crate beside us. As my strength began quickly draining away, I held on to her arm with both hands and tried pushing the gun away, but she kept pressing the trigger, until the mag was empty.

Then, as a solid wall of unconsciousness moved in to take me into a softer, dark place, I used my hundred and seventy pounds to push her down. We began squirming on the concrete. Her knees caught me in several tender places. I could feel the last of my strength vanishing.

Just as I was about to give up, I heard frantic footsteps on the concrete approaching us.

Then I blacked out.

Chapter 18

The nurse tending me was about forty, tall and extremely slender, with short red hair done in a cute pageboy. Her nametag said *OWENS*. Her long-lashed, big blue eyes said, *You're cute, baby, but awfully silly for getting yourself shot...*

Neil was standing at the foot of my bed, talking on his cell with someone from the Department. Mike stood on the other side of my bed, watching Nurse Owens tending to me and giving Neil an occasional glare. At least she hadn't been too hard on him since he'd come in a few minutes ago. For some reason, Neil wasn't his arrogant, sourpussed self. He seemed all amped up, content with life and its endless mysteries. I could tell he was impressed—in his own low-keyed, cynical way, of course—that I'd solved the case of the dead stripper. He'd also told me Davenport and Gaffman were questioning the girl who'd shot me. Neil seemed pleased about how everything came out, but I preferred to think he was just glad that I hadn't been killed.

Nurse Owens smiled and said I was doing fine. "I'll be back a little later on to check on you." Then she carefully fixed my pillow and left the room.

Neil pocketed his cell. "They found a sheet on the girl," he said.

"Let me guess. Her name isn't Lisa Randolph."

"Not bad, Deacon. Her name's Rhonda Fearing, and she's wanted in two states for embezzlement,

177

one count of accessory murder and one of aggravated assault."

"I had a feeling she wasn't a good girl when she pulled that pistol out of her bag and tried to kill me with it."

"Guess what else we found in that bag."

"Um…money?"

"Nearly half a million, to be precise."

"Fancy that," Mike said flatly.

"We traced it to Johnston's personal bank account. It was withdrawn three days ago—just about the same time the ME determined time of death when they went by to see about him."

"How'd she kill him?"

"Same as Rhodes. Throat cut."

"I guess I got off lucky."

"That ya did, my friend. By the way, you shouldn'ta gone after her by yourself. Davenport and Gaffman were right there with you. Did you forget that minor tidbit?"

"I didn't forget. I just didn't want her getting away. She's really good with disguises, and she's a champ at slipping away. I figured she had a good head-start, so I really had no choice." I gave a slight, careful shrug. Even so, the pain in my side flared up, strongly suggesting that I shouldn't move around so much.

"Good stroke of luck," Neil said. "Figuring out she was the one who approached you at Sheffield's."

"It wasn't much."

"Not from your end," Mike said with a sly grin.

"What gave her away?"

"Her smile."

"Howzat?"

I told him about the tiny dimple on her left cheek. "I remember details like that."

Neil shrugged. "Lots of babes have dimples."

"Dimples are like fingerprints," I said. "I've never seen two that look the same."

Neil looked doubtful. Then nodded. He probably decided that since I'd solved another one, arguing about some weird tactic that had helped me nail the woman would be stupid. "Good catch."

"She was also wearing super-high heels in Sheffield's. That made it kind of obvious."

He shook his head. "I really need to stop underestimating you, Deacon. Sorry. It's the cop in me. We have to be cynical. About everything."

"By this time, do we really know why she singled me out?"

Neil just smiled.

"Wanna share?"

"That was one of the first questions Davenport and Gaffman asked her. Know what she said?"

"Something tells me I'm not gonna like the answer."

"We were both right after all. She said you were alone, and closest."

"That was it?"

"She didn't want to end up in the back seat of some horny jerk's car, fighting off a group of drunks. She was looking for a quiet, unassuming guy who didn't look too sophisticated, but someone she felt she could trust. That's why she was sitting in Sheffield's for nearly three hours. Lots of jerks, but she was kinda particular. Can't blame her, can ya?"

"For thinking I'm unsophisticated? You bet I can."

"She was wrong," Mike said.

"Some people are poor judges of character," Neil said.

"Obviously. But I'd still like to think that she picked me out because of the sex thing. I do make quite an attractive figure in my best threads."

"Oh, brother…" Mike looked disgusted.

Neil sighed. "Look at it this way. If she hadn't picked you, who knows how this woulda gone down?"

"I guess you're right."

He shrugged. "Everything worked out, so why should we quibble or even question anything? Once Gillespie was scared off, Fearing realized she no longer had to share that half-mill. All she knew was that she needed to get away fast, before Gillespie thought twice about what he'd done and decided to come back for his cut. She figured that if she helped you out, you could help get her on her way. After all, you helped her the first time, right?"

"Yeah. I helped her the first time." I didn't like Neil's condescending look.

"Don't worry about it. You nailed her."

"There's that…" At least that was something. But I still didn't like being taken advantage of.

He stared at me. "By the way, any idea why Gillespie suddenly made tracks?"

"When?"

"When he had you at the storage locker and was planning to bust your bones. Bone crushers usually don't split in the middle of the program. They like to stay till the last feature. Then they slither away when their victim's unconscious or dead."

"Who knows? He seemed mental to me. A lot of these hitter types are. He spooked fairly easy."

"Probably a mental case. Good thing for you, though."

I glanced at Mike. "I've never been one to question a streak of sudden good luck."

"It *was* good luck, too. She'd already done in Johnston and made off with the bastard's cash. This time, she was looking for a scapegoat to help her get on a plane. Then she'd be out of the country in just a few hours."

"I guess she read sucker all over me. Both times."

"Well, it worked the first time, didn't it?"

"To a point."

"And we solved the case."

"Yeah, we did at that."

"What's the poop on Foreman Construction? Is it a stash house?"

"It's legit. Johnston was only a silent partner, by the way. The company's not doing very well, but that's got nothing to do with Johnston. Mismanagement seems to be their enemy."

"She lied to me about that, too."

"Anything to make her story sound better," Neil said with a shrug.

"It did that, all right. Any line on Gillespie?"

181

"We're looking for him. He won't get far."

"It would be nice if he thanked you properly," Mike said. "She would have gotten away if it hadn't been for you. And me. But we both know he'd never thank me, don't we?"

I knew better than reply to that.

Neil glanced at his watch. "Well, I gotta get back. They told me at the desk that you're gonna be fine. The slug just grazed ya. Barely nicked a rib."

"It only hurts when I laugh."

Neil shrugged. "Don't laugh."

"I'll try not to."

"And don't crack any jokes for a while."

"What do my jokes have to do with my laughing?"

"You're the only one who laughs at 'em."

"Droll, Neil."

He waved as he turned for the door. Just before he left, he paused in the doorway. "By the way, thanks."

"For what?"

"Solving the case, you moron."

"It's what I do."

Neil nodded but said nothing. Then he waved again and left.

"That was almost sweet," Mike said.

"For Neil, that *was* sweet."

"I'm really surprised he thanked you."

"You need to give him a little credit. He's got issues."

"So do you."

My cell began buzzing on my nightstand.

Careful of my side, I gingerly reached for it and glanced at it. And sighed. Then I flicked it on. "Hi, Mom."

"Ralphie, what are you doing right now?"

I knew better than tell her what was going on. I'd been lying to my mother most of my life. She'd been a worrier ever since I can remember. "Just lying around, trying to grab some shuteye. Why do you ask?"

"You sound…well, you sound like you're not feeling well."

I gawked at Mike and mouthed the words, *"How the hell does she know?"*

"She's your mother," Mike said.

I took a breath and cleared my throat. "I'm okay, Mom. How's Uncle Al?"

"That's why I called. He's doing very well, actually."

"No complications?"

"His doctor told him he's in very good shape for a man his age. He should take it easy for the next few weeks, but he saw no major issues."

"That's good to hear. I was worried."

"He did ask about you when I went to see him this morning. He asked when you were gonna come back down here for another visit."

"I'll try making it down sometime later this summer, Mom."

"That sounds good. Well, I don't want to talk long…"

"That's great, Mom." I was too tired to spar with anyone, let alone her. I wanted to take a nap.

"What's great, honey?"

"It's great that everything's fine and that Uncle Al's doing well. And you sound good, too."

She didn't reply.

"Mom?"

"Yes, dear?"

"Is something wrong?"

"I'm just worried about you, honey. You don't…well, you just don't sound like yourself."

"I'm okay. Like I said, I'm just lying around, being lazy."

"All right. I know I shouldn't worry, but I can't help it. You've been playing cowboys and Indians a long time now, and I can't help thinking that one day, you might get shot or stabbed. Or something worse."

"I'm fine, Mom. And it's cops and robbers."

"Promise me you won't get shot or anything."

"I promise."

"Good. You don't want your mother worrying, do you?"

"Not a chance, Mom."

184

Chapter 19

The hospital released me two days later.

Neil sent one of his officers from OPD to pick me up and drive me back to my condo. The officer's name was Phelps. She was about thirty-five, stacked, and totally professional. She had a cold-hearted reserve that showed in her icy blue eyes and a stiff, upright posture that told a guy that she wouldn't put up with any shenanigans.

She obviously knew she was safe with me. The numbing pain on my right side had made me look pitiful. It also did much to curb just about every conceivable urge I might consider, including my customary one-liners. I couldn't imagine saying anything that might warrant a slap in the face—which, in my present condition, would send me swiftly to the ground.

The drive from the hospital was quiet and uneventful. Officer Phelps was all business, staring straight ahead as she drove. She confined her replies to my several awkward attempts at conversation in one- or two-word bursts of dry curtness. What I gathered from her attitude was that this was merely an errand, possibly a personal favor for Neil. Nothing more. This, of course, told me that Neil had selected her personally for this job.

"She's not your type anyway." Mike said from the back seat.

I nodded.

"Anyway, she's obviously not chatty. And I don't think she'd appreciate your kind of joking around."

"You're probably right," I said without thinking.

"Pardon me?" Officer Phelps shot a quick glance at me.

"Just thinking out loud."

Without a word, she went back to her driving.

The moment she put on her blinkers to make the turn into my complex, I told her that the guard would probably give her some grief.

"No problem. I can handle this."

"Just be gentle with him. He's probably having one of his naps."

She made no further comment as she turned off Conway, pulled up to the guard's station and stopped.

The old man staggered out of his tiny building and shuffled over to her side of the cruiser. With his puffy sleep-filled eyes, he stared at her for about twenty seconds and grinned, showing off his dentures. "Howdy, ma'am…er, Officer."

She nodded politely. "I'm transporting Detective Deacon to his residence. I hope this meets with your approval."

"Huh?" He blinked. "Oh. Yeah. He…uh, lives here, don't he?"

"I assume he does if I'm transporting him here," she replied.

The guard bent, moving a little closer to her door. Then, noticing me for the first time, squinted.

"Yeah. Uh, that's him. Yup. That's Deacon." He gave me a slight wave. "What didja do this time?"

"What's that?"

"What didja do to get a police escort?"

"I got shot."

"Howzat?"

"I said I got shot."

The sleep instantly drained out of his blood-shot eyes. He turned pale. "Shot?"

"Yeah."

"How?"

"With a gun."

"Wow…"

"Maybe we proceed?" Officer Phelps sounded impatient, but her outward appearance did not change.

"Huh? Oh. Yeah, go right on ahead, Officer." He straightened and gestured for us to proceed.

"Thank you."

"Yes, ma'am." He stood stiffly as we passed.

Officer Phelps stopped outside my condo. She put the cruiser in park and switched off the ignition. Then she opened her door. "Let me help you step out."

"No, it's all right, I can manage."

Before I could finish my statement, she'd already circled the front of the cruiser, opened the passenger door, and helped me out.

I smiled, but inwardly I felt like an invalid. It didn't help matters that I was a few years older than she was, or that she could have easily pinned me to the ground. I let her lead me up the small grassy incline that took us to my front door.

I pulled my key from my pocket and unlocked my door. Then I said, "I appreciate your bringing me here, but I'm okay now."

"You're sure?"

"I'm a lot tougher than I look."

"I don't mind helping you out. You *were* shot, you know."

"It's all right. Really." I was less than a second away from telling her I didn't need tucked in. "Thanks again."

She tipped her hat, turned, and marched back down the hill, to her cruiser. I watched her as she eased away from the curb and drove back down the road that led to the complex entrance.

I closed the door and moved stiffly toward the kitchen. My supply of Jack awaited me in the cupboard above the counter. I grabbed a half-filled bottle. Then, smarting a little as I reached for a clean glass from the drainer, I saw Mike sitting on one of the barstools on the other side of the counter.

"I thought you'd left." I poured a couple of inches into the glass.

"What made you think that?"

"I don't know." I sipped the drink and immediately felt myself relaxing. "I can't see you sticking around now."

"Why shouldn't I? You're hurting. I'm waiting to see if you'll be okay."

"Thanks, but don't you need a recharge? It's been a while."

"I did a full recharge when you were passed out in the hospital."

"I guess I didn't think of that." I took my drink into the living room and collapsed on the sofa.

Mike joined me a moment later. She suddenly looked grim. "I think you should make a phone call right now."

"To who?"

"Your rude policeman buddy."

"Why Neil?"

"That Gillespie guy? The one who tried to crush your kneecap?"

"What about him?"

"They haven't found him yet."

"What's that have to do with anything?"

"They haven't found him because he's been hiding."

"That's kind of obvious, Mike." Her grim expression suddenly tapped some reality into my meds-clouded brain. "Just what are you trying to say?"

"I'm trying to tell you that I know where he's hiding."

I sat up sharply. "Where?"

"Outside. And if I were you, I'd call your friend and tell him. Officer Iceberg is still close enough to get back here in time if you call him right now."

I wasted no time fishing my cell out of my pocket.

***

Gillespie had obviously brought along a set of burglar's tools. He opened the door without a sound and appeared in the doorway, aiming his pistol and silencer at me just as I'd pocketed my cell.

"You don't seem surprised to see me." He came in and used his right foot to nudge the door shut behind him.

"Judging by the way you ran like a frightened jackrabbit from the storage facility, I would have thought you'd be in North Dakota by now."

The sudden glare in his eyes told me he obviously didn't like that. "You spooked me somehow, is all. Anyway, I'm back, and ya ain't gonna spook me again."

"What happens if you start hearing voices again?"

He blinked a few times. "Yeah, I been thinkin' about that a lot lately. Know what I came up with?"

"I can't imagine."

"See, I'd been doin' some heavy stuff that day. With the booze and all, I figure my head just wasn't on straight that day. Know what I mean?"

"In your case, yeah, I see what you mean."

"Watch it, now…"

"You asked, didn't you?"

"I've got the gun, asshole." It twitched in his hand.

"I can see it. You're not doing a very good job of hiding it."

"Got 'nads, don'tcha? Especially with a gun aimed at ya."

"Yeah, I got some serious 'nads." I was getting tired of this. I wanted to finish my drink and take a nap. I also wanted this idiot out of my apartment. I was damned particular about what sort of idiots came into my apartment. This one didn't belong here. "So tell me…what's different now?"

190

"Huh?"

"Is your head on straight?"

"Fuckin' A." He glanced about the room. His pistol didn't waver. "That's why I don't hear no voice floatin' around right now, and that's why it ain't gonna be no biggie, dustin' you. See, I heard Rhonda got hauled in, and I figure you were the one done it, right?"

"I had a little help, but yeah, that was my shtick."

He shook his head. "Bad move, Mr. Private Dick. Me and Rhonda? We were gonna hightail it with Johnston's swag, but you kinda fucked that up, didn'tcha?"

"Yeah. I guess I did at that. Sorry, but that's just how life works sometimes."

He scowled. "Kinda cocky. I'll bet you can tell I ain't gonna lower this gun pointed at your kisser."

I shrugged. "It really doesn't matter to me, one way or the other."

He grinned. With two of his lower teeth missing, it wasn't a pretty sight. "Ya really got a pair on ya. Know what I mean?"

"I've been told that a few times before."

"Well, like I said, ya kinda fucked up our plans, so I decided to head on back and let ya know just how bad ya screwed us up."

"You could have saved yourself a trip. I already figured that one out on my own."

He grinned again. "No offense, but I wanted to see the look on your face personally. Before I blew your brains clean outa your head, that is."

191

"You realize the cops are looking for you, right?"

"I kinda figured that one out. But like I said, I had to come back and letcha know how bad you messed up our plans."

I shrugged. "Couldn't help it. Your lady was trying to shoot me."

He glanced at my right side, which protruded a little from the bandages. I thought he was going to laugh. "Looks to me like she gotcha anyway. You're lucky, ya know. She's a damn good shot."

"Not good enough. Anyway, I had to stop her, didn't I? It was her fault, you know."

"What was her fault?"

"Getting caught."

"Whaddya mean?"

"She tried getting away with three cops coming at her. I guess she didn't mention that, did she? Oh, wait. She couldn't. She's in custody right now."

He was glaring. "Ya really know how to push it, don'tcha, asshole?"

"I do when I don't have much of an alternative."

He thought that one over. "Well, that don't matter none now, 'cause I'm gonna make sure ya don't fuck up anything else." He scanned the room again. "Don't look like no cops are comin' at me, does it? That cop bitch with the big jugs brought ya home is prob'ly already back at the Station by now." His pistol leveled straight at my heart.

Out of the corner of my eye, I saw Mike moving closer. But I still had to play for time. I didn't know if Officer Phelps had gotten the word from Neil yet.

"By the way… Before you shoot?"

"Howzat?"

"You just said your head was on straight, right?"

"Yeah. So?"

"That would mean you won't hear that ghost again, right?"

"Howzat?"

"I think you called her a bitch, but we'll both let that slide. For now, anyway."

"Whaddya talkin' about now, asshole?"

Still watching Gillespie, I said, "Mike, I think our friend here would like to hear your voice again."

"Hi there," she said to Gillespie. "You're not going to call me a bitch *now*, are you?"

"Mother *fuck*!" Shaking, Gillespie backed up. He popped off three quick rounds that went directly into the plaster of my dining room wall.

"You really *are* a lousy shot," she said, shaking her head.

"I hope you're good at spackling, you dumbass." I was getting really angry. His stupid impulse had just cost me close to a thousand bucks in restoration work.

His hand trembling, Gillespie kept the pistol aimed in her direction as he fumbled for the doorknob directly behind him. Once the door was open, he practically lost his balance moving around it. Then he tripped on the threshold and fell flat on his back onto the concrete slab directly in front of my door. The back of his wrist slapped the concrete, knocking the pistol from his grasp. Once he regained his senses, he rolled toward it and made a move to reach for it.

"Police! Freeze!"

Officer Phelps was standing just three feet away, her gun trained on him.

Chapter 20

The phone rang the next morning at 7:30, as I sat on the living room couch watching the beginnings of the morning sun peeking in through the horizontal blinds.

It was my friend Neil.

Luckily, I had already managed to get the coffee going. I was groggy from the meds and stiff from the throbbing pain in my side. I'd decided to pass on my morning shower. Mt morning coffee was my greatest concern. Luckily, I'd managed to get things done without making a mess.

But I wasn't quite ready for a phone call and was more than willing to give Neil a quick dose of my morning wit. "I take it you're calling because you're worried about how I'm doing since I was shot solving that case for you. I'm touched, Neil. I'm really touched."

"Can the humor, Deacon. It's entirely too early in the day for your shit. But you're right. You *are* touched."

"Good one, Neil. Did you think that one up on your own? Or did Moe, Curly or Larry say it in a film from your classic library?"

I heard him sigh and realized he was in another of his surly moods. I decided to tone down the quips a tad.

"You're right. It *is* early, and I'm not fully awake yet. Coffee's still brewing."

"Good thing this isn't exactly a courtesy call."

"What is it, then?"

195

"I'm calling to give you an update on the case."

"I take it you've gotten a confession?"

"All we had to do was put the two of 'em together."

"Fearing and Gillespie? In the same room?"

"They were both cuffed, of course, and chained to different benches, but yeah, we got it all on tape. Seems they devised the scheme to get Rhodes out of the way for Johnston and take a shitload of money from him first chance they got."

"Then it actually was Johnston's plan to do the stripper?"

"She'd been demanding more and more from him. I guess he got tired of it, so he had Gillespie do her."

"Gillespie did the deed?"

"It was Fearing. Seems Gillespie got cold feet and she stepped in."

"I guess he's more comfortable with people's kneecaps than cutting their throats. But that surprises me that the girl did it. She's much more vicious than I'd imagined."

"She had no qualms about shooting you, right?"

"I had the feeling that was a self-defense thing, but now that I'm thinking it over in my head, she seemed much too eager."

"But none of that matters since we've got the whole thing on record. Johnston and Rhodes had been pretty hot'n heavy. But when she decided to start squeezing the man's balls a little too hard, that was the last straw."

"The money thing?"

"He'd just bought her that Lexus, but yeah, it was that and the usual other stuff. You know, marry me or I'll tell everyone you're a tightwad and a crook, and like being a closet S&M pervert in your spare time."

"That's cold."

"Anyway, Johnston just didn't want to put up with that and got Gillespie to do the job."

"I take it Gillespie was a little more than just an employee?"

"Johnston obviously had some shit on Gillespie. He'd taken him on about six months ago and gave him odd jobs to do. He made it look like Gillespie was working at Foreman Construction. And since he knew all about Gillespie's record, he had the boy by the balls and could get him to do whatever he wanted."

"Where did Fearing come in?"

"She was a stripper, but she was also a prostitute. We figure Gillespie used her a couple of times and decided to keep in touch once he started working for Johnston. Who knows? Maybe he knew she was a psycho. For some guys, that's a turn-on."

"It was for me."

"When did you change your mind?"

"When I turned thirty and got shot at for the first time."

"I hear ya. Coming too close to death tends to change a man's attitude."

"Did Fearing know Rhodes before all this happened?"

"Fearing didn't come right out with it, but she did insinuate that it didn't bother her at all, doing

197

the murder, just so long as there was enough money in it for her."

"Well, she was obviously made to order with this. She must have had some sort of theatrical training. She was done up so well, I could have sworn she was Rhodes."

"Most women are real pros with makeup. They're also good at making themselves taller and bustier. Too bad she smiled at you at the hotel and gave herself away."

"You're right about that. I have what you might call a photographic memory for pretty smiles."

"Well, pretty smile or not, anyone who can slit a guy's throat like she did is a psycho."

"She made a poor choice when she picked me, though…"

"That's when Johnston's plan started crumbling. You played into Fearing's charade but became a problem when you didn't touch the car or try and open the door."

"It would have been the perfect plan. She needed a guy much younger, a lot drunker, and much hornier than I was. A college kid would have done the trick."

"Johnston was probably banking on the fact that since a stripper was involved, it would be given a lower profile. What Johnston *wasn't* banking on was that Fearing would pick a private detective out of a bar full of drunks to help in her dirty work."

"I guess I just got there at the wrong time. For her."

"And for Johnston. When he saw you outside his office, he realized something had gone very wrong. He also knew he had to do something about you, or he was going down for this. He got with Gillespie again, this time to find out more about you and what ya knew, only Gillespie messed up. Before they realized it, Johnston was having a bird over all this. When Fearing saw Johnston losing it, she panicked and did him in."

"You're positive she killed Johnston?"

"One of her prints was found on the knife handle. Perfect match."

"Careless of her."

"We figure it was a heat-of-the-moment thing."

"So she murders him and takes his money?"

"We're pretty sure Johnston promised both her and Gillespie a shitload of jack for doing in Rhodes. She figured the pot was already hers, so she took what she wanted from his office safe. There were a few bills left, but she'd picked almost all of it clean."

"I think she had the feeling Gillespie might mess things up with me, so she had another plan already in the works, this time some story that she was Johnston's stepdaughter."

"Good thing Gillespie freaked when he did."

"Good thing."

Neil went silent for a moment. "Any idea *why* he freaked?"

It was time to change the subject. "Whaddya know? My coffee's ready."

"That doesn't answer my question, smartass."

So much for that…

"My guess is, he didn't like the answers I was giving him."

I heard Neil sigh. "Then he runs away?"

"Maybe she told him what to do if he didn't get the right answers from me. This was her game, wasn't it? She was the star."

A pause. "That makes sense. She'd already got him all worked up. All she had to do was wind him up when she was ready for her grand entrance and point him in the right direction."

"How many guys do you know of haven't done something stupid because of a babe?"

"Off the top of my head? None."

"Yourself included?"

"I'll take the Fifth on that."

"Me, too. But you're right. She might have told Gillespie to work me over, but not so much that it would look like a mob thing if something went wrong, and I accidentally died. And if that didn't do the trick, he should just leave and make it look like he'd lost his patience and decided to take a break. She'd come in after a few minutes and take care of the rest using a different tactic."

"The hard thing would be finding something to make all this look legit."

"My attitude might have done it for him. Not too many have been able to take it after so long."

Neil groaned. "If anyone else had said that, I'd laugh and call 'em an idiot."

"You're all heart, Neil."

"Yeah, I've really got to do something about that. Can't have the guys at the Station taking advantage, can I?"

"One thing about all this doesn't make sense," I said after some thought. "Gillespie was in the clear.

200

He could have gotten out of the country in a day or so. Why'd he come back to kill me?"

"He mighta come back for the swag, found the girl gone, then decided to look you up and see if you knew where it was. Loose ends almost always are fatal. Especially when money and women are involved."

"Good thing Phelps wasn't far. I figure I had maybe another fifteen seconds of stalling before Gillespie shot me."

"That *was* cutting it close, wasn't it?"

"You can say that again…"

"Anyway, we got 'em. They're going down for this."

"That makes me feel much better."

"Tell me something."

"What's that?"

"Davenport's having a bird about all this. He still can't figure how you found Fearing at the hotel. He said it was kinda weird, your tracking her down with all the other activity going on at the same time. Said there were more than twenty others wandering around."

"As I told him, it was a gut instinct thing."

"You and that damn gut instinct's been driving me crazy for years."

"I'm solving cases, right?"

"That's why I really don't care much about how it's coming to ya."

"Neil, you're a smart man."

"Tell me something I don't know."

I hung up and went to pour my coffee. When I turned, I saw Mike sitting on one of the barstools on the other side of the kitchen counter.

"How long have you been sitting there?"

"A little while. Problem?"

"Never. By the way, that was Neil."

"I know."

"He just told me—"

"I heard."

"He even thanked me for—"

"You solved another case for him."

I had a sip of coffee. "Is there anything I can tell you that you don't already know?"

"Possibly, but take your time. I'm not going anywhere for a while."

"I take it you've recharged?"

"Of course."

"Maybe we can spend the afternoon quietly."

"Sounds like fun."

"Fun? Really?"

She shrugged a hazy shoulder. "I'd think you'd actually enjoy some quiet after what you've just been through."

"Now that you've mentioned it…"

"Besides, that nasty bullet wound has to mend."

"I'm sure that'll be all right."

"Eventually, but I don't want you moving around too much while you're on the mend. I really want you to take it easy this weekend. And quite possibly next week. Just to be sure."

"Now you sound like someone's mother."

"Ouch."

"You know what I meant."

"That's why I said ouch."

I went into the living room and sat down on the couch. "Mike, I could never see you as someone's mother."

"That's probably because I died before I could become one."

"That's not the reason."

"And just what *is* the reason?"

"As Doodles would say, you're a hottie. Like a firecracker. I totally agree."

"You really *are* a dog, you know."

"Woof..."

"That sounded kind of pitiful."

I shrugged. "I got shot. I hurt."

"Now that *is* pitiful."

I just smiled. Then I reached for the remote and flicked on *Law & Order*. By the time I put the remote back down and picked up my coffee cup, Mike was already sitting beside me.

Life was good.

THE END

OTHER BOOKS BY DAVID BERARDELLI

THE APPRENTICE
THE WAGON DRIVER
DEMON CHASER
THE FUNNY DETECTIVE
DEMON CHASER II
STEPPING OUT OF MY GRAVE
ESCAPE CLAUSE
FATAL INNOCENCE
JUST A SIMPLE ERRAND
COLORS
WORKING FOR A MOB BOSS
AND DARKNESS FELL
AFTER DARKNESS FELL
DEMON CHASER III
IN ANOTHER REALM
BEYOND RECOGNITION
LOOKING FOR A DEAD GUY
FAVOR FOR A FRIEND
THE NIGHTMARE COLLECTOR
HIDDEN
BEYOND GUILT
A RIPPLE IN TIME
DEMON CHASER IV

Titles available through:
Fiction4All